JANE DARROWFIELD,
PROFESSIONAL BUSYBODY

As she crept onto Route 2, Jane thought about the events at Walden Spring.

Bill Finnerty was dead. What was he doing on the golf course in the middle of the night? Did he go there willingly, or was he taken? Did he arrive at the golf course dead or alive? Most important, who killed him?

Maurice had pointed out the obvious suspect, Mike Witkowski. Mike and Bill were bitter rivals, and everyone in the community had heard Mike threaten Bill.

Jane wondered how Mike reacted when Paul took away the key to the game room. She should have asked Paul. In the literal heat of the moment, she hadn't thought of it.

Paul Peavey lied to the police about seeing Bill after dinner. A lie that had been quickly uncovered. Why had he been so reluctant to confront Bill about the tee times in the first place? And why, as Regina pointed out, had Paul brought Jane in to do his dirty work?

Karl Flagler found the body and made no bones about hating Bill. Jane had been shocked by the admission. People so rarely spoke ill of the dead. But if Karl had killed Bill, would he have admitted hating him so easily?

These were the people Jane could think of who had tangled with Bill Finnerty in her short time in the community. They, along with a couple of ghosts, were the most likely people to have killed him. . . .

Books by Barbara Ross

Published by Kensington Publishing Corporation

JANE DARROWFIELD, PROFESSIONAL BUSYBODY

Barbara Ross

KENSINGTON BOOKS
www.kensingtonbooks.com

KENSINGTON BOOKS are published by

Kensington Publishing Corp.
119 West 40th Street
New York, NY 10018

All Kensington titles, imprints, and distributed lines are available at special quantity discounts for bulk purchases for sales promotion, premiums, fund-raising, educational, or institutional use.

Special book excerpts or customized printings can also be created to fit specific needs. For details, write or phone the office of the Kensington Sales Manager: Attn.: Sales Department. Kensington Publishing Corp., 119 West 40th Street, New York, NY 10018. Phone: 1-800-221-2647.

Kensington and the K logo Reg. U.S. Pat. & TM Off.

First Printing: July 2019
ISBN-13: 978-1-4967-2449-6
ISBN-10: 1-4967-2449-6

ISBN-13: 978-1-4967-1995-9 (ebook)
ISBN-10: 1-4967-1995-6 (ebook)

10 9 8 7 6 5 4 3 2

Printed in the United States of America

This book is dedicated to Lea Wait and Bob Thomas. Friends, indeed.

Chapter One

"You're a hard person to get ahold of."

The face of the young man sitting on the other side of her desk swam into view. Jane's glasses were new. The cheery optometrist had assured her she could shift easily from gazing out her back window into her garden to working on her computer to watching television. She'd get used to them in no time. No time at all. But after more than a week, the glasses still gave the whole world an underwater feel, which, while not unpleasant, could hardly have been their aim.

The young man shifted on the hard wooden chair, placing a slim ankle on his knee. He had short brown hair and wore tortoiseshell-rimmed glasses. He was conservatively dressed in a light-blue seersucker suit, something one hardly saw these days. Conservative, except for his socks, which were yellow with bright blue fish cavorting across them. The socks, Jane thought, made the man.

"I'm sorry I didn't return your earlier messages," Jane said. "I didn't comprehend what you were after. I still don't."

"Hello," the phone message had said. "This is Paul Peavey from Walden Spring, the lifecare community for active adults fifty-five plus in Concord, Massachusetts. Irma Brittleson recommended you. Can you give me a call, please? Our number is—"

Jane had run in from her garden to answer the blasted cell phone, which she'd left on her desk. As she'd listened to the message, she'd tried to conjure the kind of postapocalyptic world that would be required for her to return this call, but she could not. Would she ever get so desperate for the sound of a human voice she'd let someone try to sell her a condominium in an old folks village? She hoped not. And what was the story with her great and good friend Irma, giving her name and cell phone number to this guy? Did she think Jane could no longer handle her own home?

Jane had ignored the second message as well. Which is why, she supposed, Paul Peavey had navigated the flagstones of the walk that ran along the side of her Cambridge, Massachusetts, home and knocked on the door to her office, which was a converted back porch.

Peavey attempted to explain. "As I said, Mrs. Darrowfield, Miss Brittleson gave me your name. I'm the executive director at Walden Spring, the community for active adults fifty-five plus in Concord—"

"Mr. Peavey—"

"Paul."

"Paul, I'm sorry Irma wasted your time. I am not the least in the market for—"

"No, no, no. I'm not selling anything. In fact, I'm hoping to buy something. Your time, that is. To buy your time."

A most unexpected remark.

"Miss Brittleson comes to Walden Spring frequently to visit a friend. We got to talking, and she told me about some of the things you've done to . . . um . . . intervene, I guess would be the word, and fix some potentially awkward or even tragic situations. When she told me about you, I thought, that's exactly what we need. We need someone to intervene and fix something in our community."

Jane was intrigued. And flattered, in a vague sort of way, though she wondered what Irma had been telling people. "When you say 'fix something,' Mr. Peavey—"

"Paul."

"Paul, what exactly are you referring to?"

"We're having some issues, hmm, with the, uh, social dynamics in the community."

Social dynamics? "Could you be more specific?"

"I think it's better for you to come and see for yourself. Say about ten a.m. Monday?"

"Aren't there social workers or therapists who specialize in this sort of thing?"

"Been there. Done that. No results. I need someone like you, who can come into the community and get actively involved. I need someone who will *intervene.*"

Curiouser and curiouser. "When you said you wanted to buy my time, what did you mean?"

"I assumed I would pay your hourly fee. Whatever it is."

"I charge eight hundred dollars a day." Jane hoped Paul Peavey didn't notice the flush that crept up her neck. She had never asked for that sum of money before. She had never asked for any money before, when people had asked her to intervene. She was deeply skeptical about Peavey's offer and hoped by naming the largest sum she dared, he would have second thoughts.

He did not. "Fine, fine." Peavey stood, leaning across the desk to shake her hand. "Ten o'clock Monday, then?"

"Let me check my calendar. I'll call to confirm later this afternoon." There was nothing on her calendar for Monday morning. Of that Jane was certain. But she needed time to think Peavey's offer through.

"Thank you. I look forward to hearing from you."

Jane escorted the young man to the multipaned glass door of the old porch and watched him head down the walk. "My goodness," she said as he retreated. "There's a new one." She glanced at the time on her phone and picked her pocketbook up off the desk. She didn't have time to consider the young man's proposition right away. She had to hotfoot it around the corner to Helen Graham's house or she'd be late for bridge.

"And this man wants to pay you?" Across the bridge table, Phyllis Goldstein arched an eyebrow at Jane.

"Wants to pay you for what?" Helen Graham entered through her swinging kitchen door, posture perfect, her hair in the pageboy she had worn since Jane had met her thirty-nine years earlier. She placed a tray laden with a pitcher of cold tea, tall glasses filled with ice cubes, lemon wedges, and sweeteners on the sideboard in the living room.

"That's the rub," Jane answered. "I'm not exactly certain for what. Something about a problem at Walden Spring, the over-fifty-five community in Concord he's in charge of."

"So Paul did phone you." Irma Brittleson spoke from the vestibule inside Helen's front door. The windows and tiled floor in the tiny space added an echoey quality to her voice. She'd let herself in, as they all had. It was a ritual, no matter which of their homes they played in. The last to arrive was responsible for latching the door.

"Phoned and came by," Jane answered.

"Good. I'm glad he took my recommendation."

Jane shifted her chair to face Irma. "Why did you send him to me?"

"Because—"

"Goodness, we're getting ahead of ourselves." Helen had returned from the kitchen with a plate of chocolate cookies, fresh from the oven, smelling like heaven. "Let's play cards."

The women sat, the cards were dealt. The day was warm, but happily the humidity was low, and a breeze moved the sheer curtains in Helen's first-floor windows.

"News of the Week in Review," Phyllis said, in

another tradition as old as the game. "Hostess first."

Helen spoke, as she always did, about her husband, Hugh, and her children. Her older two were married, the parents of a brood of grandchildren. Helen's third child, Lizzie, was thirty and single. Lizzie's engagement to a most unsuitable man had been originally responsible for Jane's growing reputation as someone who could help out with problems that, while vexing or frightening, weren't appropriate for the police or other authorities. When Helen had described Lizzie's fiancé as "dead behind the eyes," Jane, who'd been a little at sea after her retirement, decided to investigate. It hadn't taken much to find his other two fiancées and his "late" mother living on the other side of Cambridge. Jane had been the one to warn him off, too, reasoning it was better that he break Lizzie's heart sooner rather than run her through the wood chipper later. Helen had been grateful, and she had talked. A lot.

Jane's reputation had grown. All winter and spring, people had made their way down the flagstone walk to Jane's office.

Gerri McLaughlin needed help switching from her hairdresser to the one in the next chair. During an unexpected absence, the other hairdresser had done Gerri's cut and color. The resulting hairdo had a new bounce and shine that had added a bounce to Gerri's step as well. She'd urged her original hairdresser to re-create it, but without success.

Every woman knew ending a relationship with the person who did your hair was fraught. It was a professional arrangement, one in which money was paid for skill and services. But it was also a relationship in which confidences were exchanged and loyalty expected. Turning up a month later in the next chair was unthinkable. Gerri had considered proposing to the new hairdresser that she sneak into the shop after hours but had rejected it as ridiculous.

Jane counseled directness. It was time for a change. Not just in style but in stylist. When Gerri couldn't face it, Jane had gone in and delivered the message herself. The original hairdresser was hurt but accepted the switch as inevitable. It was better, after all, to keep the client in the shop. Gerri had reported that after a couple of tense appointments, with much sighing coming from the next chair, everything had evened out. Everyone was fine.

Virginia Westbury didn't know how to tell her neighbors their five-year-old was peeing in her garden every day. Jane volunteered to weed Virginia's garden for a while. When the boy approached, equipment at the ready, so to speak, she jumped up and yelled, "Cut it out! You *know* you're not supposed to do that!" He screamed and ran home. Jane worried about what he might tell some future therapist about the encounter, but the peeing stopped and Virginia was happy.

In Jane's opinion, many people sadly lacked the skill to have difficult conversations with acquaintances and neighbors. Given a noisy house party or a car parked blocking a driveway, people stewed in silence—or worse, called the police—when a simple knock on the door and a polite request would have done the job. It was into this breach that Jane

had leapt again and again. Now she was being offered the chance to be paid for her efforts. Why
wouldn't she take it?

When Helen was done speaking, Irma Brittleson reported on her week. Irma was retired from
her job as a top administrator at Mount Auburn
Hospital, but she still volunteered there several
days a week. She lived with her mother in a lovely
two-family overlooking a park on the Cambridge–
Somerville line.

Irma had also sought Jane's help, and brought
her first failure. Irma's ninety-six-year-old mother,
the irrepressible Minnie, had been scammed quite
badly by someone who had telephoned, claiming
to be from her bank, asking her to help test their
procedures by withdrawing $9,000 from her inac-
tive savings account and then returning it to the
bank manager, who would be waiting in the lobby.
Minnie, happy to help, had struggled down her
front steps while Irma was at her volunteer job and
taken a cab to the bank.

The bank manager was, of course, not the bank
manager, and the money was gone.

Jane had explained this was not a job for her
but for the police. When Minnie refused to involve
the authorities because she was mortified, Jane
had volunteered to report Minnie's story for her.

All this had occurred at a time when Jane was
experimenting with letting her hair go gray. When
she told the nice Detective Alvarez of the Cambridge Police Fraud Squad, the story "about a
friend," he had assumed *she* was the ninety-six-year-
old Minnie.

Horrified, Jane had set him straight, left the police station, and raced immediately to her salon, where the redoubtable Hugo had returned her hair to the honey-blond that, while not natural to nature, felt natural to Jane. "I told you it would never work," Hugo had said.

"Back to you, Jane," Phyllis said when Irma finished the report on her week. "Who is this guy you were talking about, and what does he want to pay you for?"

"As I said earlier, he's the executive director at Walden Spring," Jane repeated. "Irma recommended me."

The three of them looked at Irma, who shrugged. "He told me he needed help with some community problems." She looked at Jane. "That's what you do, isn't it?"

Was it?

"When is this happening, if you do it?" Phyllis asked. Phyllis's face was soft and pleasant, like the rest of Phyllis. She was short and kind, a retired attorney and mother of four.

"Mr. Peavey wants me to meet him at Walden Spring on Monday morning."

"No!" Phyllis shouted, too loud.

"Why ever not?" Jane was slightly annoyed Phyllis would presume to tell her what she could or couldn't do. Advice was fine, but edicts, not so much.

"Because Monday is the day you're going to help me find a man to date," Phyllis answered.

Only Irma had the nerve to say what they were all thinking. "You're kidding."

Phyllis had had a long and happy marriage to Sam, a real sweetheart, who'd been struck down by leukemia at the age of fifty-nine. That was tragic. Also tragic was Phyllis's reaction. Less than a year after Sam's death, over the boisterous objections of her grown children and the somewhat more muted ones from the bridge club, Phyllis had married Craig, shortly thereafter known as "The Awful Craig," and finally just as "The Awful."

Phyllis was sparkly and pretty. She was round like a snowman, round hips, round chest, and a round face she emphasized with her short, feathered brown hair, a color that was no more natural than Jane's honey-blond but that suited her. Phyllis's was the kind of roundness men found enticing, and when Jane went out with her, she couldn't help noticing Phyllis still attracted their attention.

Phyllis had gone to law school when her youngest child started kindergarten and later made so much money as a corporate lawyer, both she and Sam were astonished. But like many smart people, Phyllis could be incredibly dumb.

It had taken two years for Phyllis to admit her marriage to The Awful was a disaster. She ordered him out of her house. He refused to go. Phyllis hired a divorce attorney. The Awful did, too. Delays piled on delays.

Phyllis moved in with Jane and had the electricity and the gas turned off at her house. She let the oil tank run dry. At first, she drew the line at turning off the water, fearful of what The Awful could do in a house without functioning toilets, but as summer turned to fall and fall to winter, and the possibility of burst pipes turned to a probability, Phyllis had the city turn the water off at the street and a plumber drain the system.

It took a few weeks after that, but one morning The Awful Craig was gone. His lawyer, who'd dragged his heels for months, suddenly agreed to everything. Craig was marrying again.

That had been a year ago. So when Phyllis announced she wanted to date, the rest of the bridge group had their reservations.

"Why are you staring at me?" Phyllis asked. "I won't make the same mistake twice. I was crazy with grief last time. Besides," she added triumphantly, "Jane is going to make sure I don't. She's going to meet all my dates before I go out with them." Phyllis looked at Jane. "I will date only the ones she preapproves."

Phyllis's announcement that Jane would be screening her dates was met with a fair number of objections, most of them Jane's.

"How do you know there will even be dates to approve?" Jane asked.

"Because I signed up for an Internet dating service, and I don't mind telling you, there's been a lot of interest."

"And what makes you think these men will agree to talk with me before they even meet you?" Jane pressed.

"Because I posted a profile for you on the service, too. They'll agree to date you, and after you sort through them, you'll introduce me to the winner." Phyllis sat back, triumphant, while the other three stared with their mouths open.

"Phyllis, I cannot believe you signed me up for an online dating service without so much as asking." *Really, this was too much.*

"It was easy. I had plenty of photos of you. I

know your likes and dislikes, though I did mix in some of my own to make sure we could attract the same men."

"And what made you think I'd agree to this?" Jane's tone was sharper than she meant it to be. Phyllis had been through hell.

"You helped Helen. You tried to help Minnie. Why wouldn't you help me? We're friends."

Good grief. How could Jane even argue? No wonder Phyllis was such a good attorney.

Back at home, Jane sat at the breakfast bar in her kitchen and powered up her laptop. Her photo beamed out from the top of the Getadate.com profile Phyllis had created. Jane had to admit, she'd picked a good one. It had been taken at her retirement party, hair done (then and now again, expensively, honey-blond), makeup on, the pacific blue of a beautiful silk jacket bringing out the blue of her eyes.

In combination, she had to admit she and Phyllis were quite the catch. She'd listed their interests: gardening and travel (Jane's), along with gourmet cooking and golf (Phyllis's) and, of course, bridge (both). She'd left off a few hobbies, such as watching trashy daytime television (Phyllis's) and butting into other people's lives (now apparently Jane's).

There had been, as Phyllis said, plenty of interest. Jane scanned the profiles of Phyllis's potential dates, who were, as her (and Jane's) preference requested, all men between the ages of 60 and 75. True to their mutual zip code, the men were professors, consultants, doctors, lawyers, and businessmen. Most were divorced, a few widowed. Many said they were retired, though others said they were "still working, though it's not the center of my world," perhaps unwittingly explaining the reason their earlier marriages had failed.

Their listed interests were pack-like: current events, sports, hiking, music. So many of them claimed a love of art it seemed that Internet dating should be unnecessary. If what they wrote were true, every gallery and museum in the Boston area would be packed with eligible men 24-7.

A surprising number had indicated their grown children lived with them. Given the men's ages, these children were most likely in their thirties. Jane wondered if this was some sort of trend—men who didn't live with their children when they were young now housing them long past their sell-by dates. Or perhaps these men were living in their children's homes. Either way, Phyllis had wisely ruled these candidates out.

Phyllis had been busy indeed. Jane had four coffee dates lined up at forty-five-minute intervals on Monday afternoon at Peet's Coffee in Harvard Square. There had never really been a question of whether Jane would help Phyllis. Of course she would. The bridge players were her oldest and dearest friends. She would do anything for them. Almost.

Jane printed the profiles and made notes on them much as she would have annotated a résumé before an interview with a job candidate. If Agatha Christie's Miss Marple understood the whole of human behavior from observing the citizens of the village of St. Mary Mead, Jane had gained her skills toiling in the bowels of corporate America. Offices were like villages in so many ways, and the art of managing people was, in the end, the art of understanding what motivated them.

Prepared for the dates, Jane checked out Walden Spring. The photos on its website showed groups of smiling seniors, the very definition of "active adults 55+." People with white hair but improbably perfect skin swung golf clubs, swam in an indoor pool, laughed over a card game, and tucked into gorgeous plates of food in a dining room that looked like it belonged in an expensive country club. Another page of the website showed the floor plans of the various units. Jane didn't spend much time on them. There was no real information about the cost, just a discrete request to call or e-mail for more information. But it couldn't be cheap. Not in that location, and not with all those services.

Jane glanced at the console phone on her desk, still hooked up the landline. She owed Paul Peavey an answer.

It had been thirteen months since Jane had "taken the package" (an expression that always made her think of a spy swallowing cyanide) and retired as a senior vice president at one of the mutant children of the company that was known, when she joined it, as Ma Bell. Retirement had come earlier than expected, but she'd heeded the advice of her long-dead great-aunt, who said, "Always take cookies when cookies are passing." The subsequent rounds of layoffs and the diminishing amounts of the inducements confirmed this bit of wisdom.

In the months since Jane had retired, she'd

cleaned out her closets, the basement, and the attic. She'd organized her photographs chronologically, her spices categorically, and her books alphabetically, by author. She'd traveled to Florence, Siena, and the Amalfi Coast. She'd planted a hosta garden on the shady side of the house, along the path Paul Peavey had trod to her office door that morning.

She exalted in her new freedoms. She didn't set her alarm clock. She gave her corporate clothes to charity. In other words, she had done the things she'd dreamed of doing during all those years at work.

She'd stopped herself when she began sticking acid-free labels on the bottoms of her most precious possessions, explaining what they were; where they had come from; and why Jonathan, her only son and heir, should keep them. Trying to control him even from the grave, he would bitterly complain when the time came. *Enough*, she told herself. *You're not dead yet.* If actuarial tables were any guide, she had twenty more years, a quarter of a lifetime.

The "favors" she had done for friends and neighbors, the little problems she had solved, had filled in her time. She had received flowers, pies, and breads, and even the occasional bottle of bubbly, but no one had thought to pay her.

Jane's retirement was a comfortable one. With stubbornness and luck she'd recovered from the financial disaster that had come decades ago with the end of her marriage. A lot of her wealth was in her house; her neighborhood had gone from solid to insanely expensive in the forty years she'd lived there. At some point, the house might have to go, to get the equity out or because she could no longer handle the stairs. Perhaps a place like Walden Spring loomed in her future. But for now, she was fine.

Still, there was a precariousness that came, not so much with retirement but with age. After she had dug herself out from the debt her husband's exit had created, she had always said to herself, *If I have to, I can do anything. I can wait on tables. I can work in retail. I can* . . . The list was endless. But now that wasn't so certain. Even if she had the strength and stamina required to do those jobs, would anyone hire her?

Paul Peavey had offered to pay her a good sum. A very tidy sum. Why wouldn't she take him up on it?

Before she left her office, Jane called and left a message on Peavey's office phone. She would be there Monday at ten. She also called Phyllis.

"All right. I'll help you screen your dates."

"Of course you will. The first one's at two o'clock on Monday at Peet's. Don't be late."

Chapter Two

At a little before ten on Monday, Jane pulled her sturdy, orange Volvo, known as Old Reliable, into the private road that led to Walden Spring. The complex stood high on a hill surrounded by woods and a golf course. Despite her reflexive dislike for these kinds of faux communities, Jane begrudgingly admitted the setting was attractive. She drove up the winding road and parked in one of the spots marked Visitor. A wide walk led through a two-story archway in the building that bordered the parking lot. She had no idea what to expect.

Jane been a bit flummoxed about how to prepare for the meeting. She'd updated her résumé, such as it was, constructing a sanitized version of her "cases" in elevated corporate-speak. The hairdresser switch became "supplier reorganization," and the peeing five-year-old became a problem of "inappropriate territoriality and boundary violation."

It would have helped if she'd known what to do about the "community problems" once she got to Walden Spring. She thought her way through all the vapid morale-building seminars she'd gone through with the phone company. Nothing seemed to apply. She didn't think she could stage trust falls with a group so prone to osteoporosis.

Although Peavey had appeared to hire her on the spot, she assumed he had other people he needed to account to—a board of directors or some far-off corporate owners—for the kind of expense she'd proposed, if the job lasted more than even a few days.

She'd taken care with dressing and grooming, too. Should she treat the meeting like a job interview, her first in more than thirty-five years, or should she try to "blend in" with the community? And, given the range of dress she'd seen worn by her age cohort in the wild, what did "blend in" mean?

In the end, she'd compromised, donning a khaki skirt and canvas flats, but paired with a crisp, pink blouse she could have comfortably worn to her old job. She put on lipstick and left the annoying new progressive glasses on her bedside table. She put on sunglasses but tucked an old pair of readers into her purse, in case she was called upon to review or sign some kind of contract. Satisfied, but still nervous, she'd headed out the door.

At Walden Spring, she stopped on the other side of the archway to take in the view. Two long, four-story apartment buildings formed an L-shape around a large, rectangular lawn with paths running through it. The green space had a lovely campus-y feel. On the third side of the rectangle, a free-standing building had a sign over its doorway that read, CLUBHOUSE. The fourth side of the lawn was open to the golf course.

Just inside the archway, she found the management office. Jane entered an ample reception room and knocked lightly on the open door to the only office. Paul Peavey stood up from behind his enormous mahogany desk and greeted her warmly.

"Mrs. Darrowfield—"

"Jane."

"Welcome." He motioned for her to sit and got down to business. She'd expected he would give her more background about her assignment. Instead, Peavey started right in, as if the deed were done.

"I think Mrs., um, Jane, the best thing to do is to treat you like a prospective buyer. It's common for people who are considering purchasing at Walden Spring to move into one of our guest units and spend a little time getting a feel for the community and what it has to offer. I've asked our realtor to take you on a tour as she would any other prospect. She doesn't know why you're here."

"Move in?" Jane was nonplussed. The idea had never occurred to her. "I'm terribly sorry. I wasn't planning to move in."

"But you must. I don't think you'll get to the bottom of it if you don't."

Avoidance seemed like the best tactic. She'd tell

him she wasn't moving in after she had something to report. "Can you tell me more about your problems? Get to the bottom of what?"

Peavey looked uncomfortable. "I think there's a natural tendency in humans to gravitate to people who are like us, people who have similar interests and values."

"That hardly sounds like a problem."

"It's not. But when there is hostility between groups of people, it can create a lot of tension and unhappiness."

"Hostility?"

"Yes. You know, rivalries." Now he looked not just uncomfortable but unhappy.

"Are you telling me you have gangs at Walden Spring?" For a moment, Jane flashed to a chorus line of elderly Sharks and Jets, snapping arthritic fingers and singing.

"Certainly we do not have a gang problem. I think it's best for you to see for yourself." Paul punched the numbers on his phone and then spoke into it. "Can you come over now?" After he hung up, he turned back to Jane. "Regina Campbell is our in-house realtor. She handles all our properties at Walden Spring."

A few moments later, Regina strode through the door. She was broad-shouldered and tall, towering in her high heels. In her late twenties, professionally dressed, she had a pretty face framed by brown hair curling to below her shoulders.

"After you take Mrs. Darrowfield around to see the properties," Paul told Regina, "could you give her a tour of the clubhouse and perhaps leave her there for lunch?"

"Lunch on her own? In the dining room? We don't usually—" Regina seemed more than reluctant.

"Yes, please, Regina. I'm sure Jane will be fine."

For the next hour, Jane and Regina toured the model apartments of Walden Spring. Patiently, Jane let Regina show off the granite countertops, the Jacuzzis in the master baths, and the large balconies overlooking the quad and the golf course beyond.

The two-bedroom models, the Emerson and the Alcott, appeared to be mirror images of one another. The smaller units were called the Hawthorne and the Thoreau. When Jane told Regina she expected the Thoreau to be a single room with no heat, the realtor stared at her blankly. Surely it couldn't have been the first time she'd heard that joke. The Thoreau was the smallest of the units, just one bedroom, but turned out to be very nice. Open plan, spacious kitchen with plenty of storage, light and airy throughout.

The apartment buildings had multiple entranceways, which meant only eight units shared each small foyer and elevator bank. As they walked from one unit to another, Regina and Jane used a wide path that ran around the perimeter of the quad. People seemed to have golf carts to haul their groceries from the parking lot to the entrances to their buildings and generally to get around the complex.

"What's that?" Jane pointed to a medium-sized

building, more institutional looking than the rest
of the complex. It sat a ways down a narrow paved
roadway between the golf course and the woods.

"The long-term care facility," Regina said quickly,
as though she preferred to talk about anything else.
"And of course, we do all the maintenance for your
unit," Regina prattled on, keeping to her script.
"No more cleaning gutters or shoveling snow."

The more Regina talked, the more appealing
Jane found the whole idea of living in a place like
Walden Spring. Like most houses in Cambridge,
hers had no garage, and for close to forty winters
she'd scraped ice off a succession of cars and dug
them out of snowdrifts.

Why am I so determined to keep my house, Jane wondered. It was too big, now, certainly. Perhaps it had
always been too big, even when three of them lived
there. After her husband left, all she could think
was, *I must keep the house, I must keep the house, I must
keep the house.* Of course, she wanted Jonathan to
stay in the same school, keeping his life as stable as
she could while his parents' problems swirled
around him like flakes in a shaken snow globe.
And Jane's friends, her bridge group, lived nearby.
What would have become of her in those first terrifying months without their support, their humor,
their love? And during all the years that followed.

They had almost reached the clubhouse, Regina
chattering the whole time about the "amenables."
The clubhouse was built on a slope, so they entered
on the second floor. A balcony overlooked the tables of the empty dining hall. From below came
the tinkle of glasses and cutlery and the aroma of
lunch being prepared. A two-story wall of windows

faced the golf course. There were no white table-cloths, no formal place settings on the tables. Perhaps that was reserved for dinner, or a mere fantasy for the Walden Spring website.

Three doorways, widely spaced, ran along the back wall of the balcony. Regina guided Jane to the first one. Inside, music boomed from an iPod dock. A group of fit-looking women and men who had left fifty-five years well behind were doing the Funky Chicken. There were some scary spandex costumes along with some nearly see-through yoga pants in that room. The woman who was leading didn't look any younger than the group at large.

"Very impressive," Jane commented. Cambridge was a walking city, and she relied on that, plus her garden work, for exercise.

In the next room, classical music played softly and a dozen or so people wearing smocks stood at easels painting a fruit bowl that stood on a center table. It seemed like a happy, focused group. A familiar-looking woman with a head full of lavender ringlets and bright blue eyes smiled from behind the easel nearest the door. Jane smiled back tentatively. The face seemed familiar, but Jane couldn't place her.

The third room had two billiards tables and a poker table in its center, and flat-screen TVs hooked to video consoles were along one wall. A group of men, most wearing black leather jackets, were hanging out. Two played pool while six others played cards. In the corner, a man dressed entirely in black—jeans, T-shirt, and leather jacket—hung his head out the window.

"Mike! Mike!" Regina's tone was sharp. "See

that sign? NO SMOKING. How many times do we have to tell you? And Leon in here with his oxygen. You could get us all killed!"

Mike threw his butt out the window and turned to look at the interlopers. His gray hair was greased back. "Sorry, ma'am," he mumbled. Someone at the poker table laughed.

"Let's go see the dining room." Regina led Jane down a flight of stairs and unlocked the door to the dining hall with a keycard. "Lunch is cafeteria-style, dinner is table service. Stay if you like." Her look conveyed this wasn't a good idea and she wouldn't have left Jane there if Paul hadn't insisted. Regina handed over a brochure and a business card.

"Who comes to the dining room?" Jane asked. "Every unit you showed me had a huge kitchen."

Regina laughed. "People think they'll use those kitchens, but they never do. The single people like to have company for meals, and the married women . . . they're just so thrilled not to have to come up with something for dinner for the millionth night of their lives. Everybody basically eats all their meals here at the clubhouse."

On some silent cue, a sound like a stampede of sensible shoes filled the hallway behind the door.

"Gotta run!" Regina sprinted out the door that led to the golf course at the same moment a man dressed in white unlocked the main door and the hordes descended.

*　　*　　*

The dining hall was in chaos. All Walden Spring arrived at once, some aided by canes and some by walkers or wheelchairs. The first group through the main door was a gaggle of deeply tanned, hard-haired women. It looked as if they had looted a Lilly Pulitzer resort wear store and then dressed in everything they'd stolen. The similarity of cut and color in their clothes gave the effect of a uniform.

At the same moment, three golf carts pulled up to the outside door. The men in the carts jumped out and entered the cafeteria, mixing with the Lilly Pulitzer group, plaid pants clashing with the signature bright pinks and greens of the Pulitzer dresses. Somehow, they all ended up at the front of the line, and the other residents queued behind them. The artists whom Jane had seen earlier came in chattering with the dancers in their neon spandex. The leather jacket crew followed on their heels.

Jane stood for a few moments taking it all in, then dumped the brochure Regina had given her in the trash and got into the endless line.

By the time she had lunch on her tray, everyone was seated. Jane stood in the center of the room, considering what to do. She could sit at a table by herself, but that wouldn't help her find whatever it was Paul Peavey wanted her to discover. She was looking around when someone called "Yoo-hoo!" over the din. The lavender-ringleted woman from the art room. "Jane! Come sit with us," she called.

Evangeline Murray, that's who the striking woman was. She and Irma Brittleson were great friends, and Jane had met Evangeline a few times in casual gatherings at Irma's house. She must have been the person Irma was visiting when she'd recommended Jane to Paul Peavey.

Jane made her way to the pushed-together tables in the corner of the cafeteria, where the besmocked artists and the spandex-covered dancers were eating and laughing.

"Are you considering Walden Spring?" Evangeline asked after Jane sat and introductions had been made.

"I'm thinking about it," Jane answered. "Do you like it here?"

"Love it. Best thing I ever did."

"Was it hard giving up your home?" Jane's question was genuine.

"Horrible," Evangeline answered. "I sorted and cried, cried and sorted. I cried an ocean of tears and threw out a boatload of stuff. Worst pain I ever went through. But now it's gone, and I've never felt lighter. I have as much room as I need. I have great company, and I'm busy every day. I don't have to mow grass or shovel snow or clean gutters. And I don't have to worry about dropping dead somewhere and leaving my poor heirs to make head or tail of all that stuff."

"It's the home equivalent of wearing clean underwear in case you wind up in the ER," Jane said. "Your underdrawers and your desk drawers are clean in case of the unexpected."

"I couldn't have put it better myself. You'll love it here, too. I can tell."

"Just remember to keep your head down and stay out of the crossfire," interjected a tall, skinny man wearing a black beret, black pants, a black polo shirt, and a black blazer. He sat next to Evangeline.

"Keep my head down? What crossfire?"

"Ignore Maurice. He always looks at the dark side," Evangeline responded.

"I do not!" Maurice was indignant. "I'm just saying." He was craggy-faced, with large features— large, brown, expressive eyes; prominent nose; large mouth.

"Who are they?" Jane nodded at the couple holding court at the center of the Lilly Pulitzer/plaid pants table. He was a bantam rooster of a man with a thick crop of dark hair. Jane had noticed him in the cafeteria line. He was short but moved like a much larger man with his chest puffed out and a bit of a swagger. The luxuriant hair must have been an asset when he was young, and now worked even more magic, surrounded as he was by the follicly challenged. She was petite and very tan. Her face was wrinkle-free and frozen, as if she were already embalmed. Her hair didn't move when her head did. In fact, it didn't move at all.

Evangeline rolled her eyes. "Bill Finnerty and Doris Milner. Doris is a widow. Bill's wife's over in the long-term care facility."

"Alzheimer's," the pretty dancer sitting across from Jane whispered.

"I hear she's fakin' it just to get a break from being married to that jerk," Maurice added.

"Maurice!" Evangeline colored. "What an awful thing to say."

"How sad for Mr. Finnerty," Jane said.

"Sad for us," Maurice corrected. "He takes his aggression out on innocent golfers and anyone else who disturbs his sensibilities."

Jane looked around the dining hall and suddenly was overwhelmed by a feeling of déjà vu. The golf jocks sitting with the expensively dressed popular girls. The leather-jacketed bad boys with the greased-back hair. The tables full of couples. The lonely people sitting by themselves, staring at their trays. The dancers and the artists in the corner, Jane sitting among them. She had thought her corporate experience was what she brought to this assignment. But now it was obvious. Walden Spring was high school.

"Who disturbs Bill's sensibilities?" Jane asked.

"Like Mike Witkowski over there." Maurice gestured to the man in black who'd been smoking in the billiard room. He held court at the leather jacket table and didn't seem to have a care in the world. "Bill hates Mike. And vice versa. So Bill rules the golf course and Mike runs the game room. Nobody can use either area unless they're in the right crowd."

"That's why I took up dancercise," one of the men at the table said. "I haven't been able to get a tee time all summer."

"None of us go in the game room. There are some great exercise games on those video players in there, and I'd love to use them, but that's Mike's territory," the pretty woman who'd led the dance class added.

"And Doris thinks someone died and made her Queen of Walden Spring," Evangeline huffed.

"They're all making our lives miserable," Maurice said.

At that moment, Mike Witkowski stood and bussed his tray, walking close, very close, behind where Bill and Doris were seated. Mike's tray tilted, ever so slightly, a devilish glint in his eye. A glass tipped to its side and rolled, sprinkling liquid on Bill's beautiful head of hair.

Bill jumped up and grabbed Mike by the T-shirt. Mike's tray clattered to the floor. The next minute Bill and Mike were rolling on the ground. The other plaid-pants guys rushed toward them, while the leather-jackets stood on the perimeter, lobbing dessert items into the melee.

"FOOD fight!" someone yelled.

"Oh, Lord." Maurice sighed. "Here we go again."

Outside, another golf cart pulled up, and four burley men in groundskeepers' uniforms jumped out and ran toward the fight. Everyone else headed for the exits as fast as they could go, which in some cases wasn't very.

Evangeline grabbed Jane by the arm and pulled her toward the main stairwell. The press of the crowd going up the stairs took Jane's breath away. She had a vision of a slow-motion soccer riot. When they got to the top of the stairs, Jane didn't stop. The high school feeling had unsettled her. She bid Evangeline and Maurice a hasty farewell and hustled out of the clubhouse. Paul Peavey hurried past, headed for the melee. Jane put her thumb to her mouth, pinky to her ear, and mouthed, "I'll call you." She continued straight to Old Reliable, started the engine, and peeled out of the Walden Spring parking lot.

She was almost to the end of the long, winding drive, safe in the real world, when earsplitting noise surrounded her. Mike Witkowski and his gang pulled their motorcycles up on either side of her car and then roared past. There were eight of them. Nine if you counted Leon with his oxygen tank, riding in Mike's sidecar.

Chapter Three

Jane was almost late to her Getadate meetings that afternoon at Peet's. When she'd jumped into Old Reliable in the Walden Spring parking lot, she noticed a scary-looking white glob on the shoulder of her good, pink blouse that had mercifully turned out to be vanilla pudding, a consequence of the food fight. By the time she'd stopped at home to change and found a place to park in always congested Harvard Square, she had to hustle to get to the coffee shop before the first Getadate did.

She ordered her decaf coffee drink as soon as she got inside, so there wouldn't be any weirdness about who paid. The coffee ordering always seemed unnecessarily complex but the petite, dark-haired barista was a pro who deftly guided Jane through the process. She gave Jane an ear-to-ear grin as she handed over the steaming cup.

Jane settled at a table in the middle of the room, in a seat facing the door, and then checked her phone for the list of date names Phyllis had sent her.

It took a few moments for Jane to recognize Calvin Marquart, but she felt she could be excused because the photo on his profile had been taken at least twenty years earlier. And he was hidden behind his giant mobility scooter.

He spotted her and drove straight to her table. "I'll be honest," he said before introducing himself and at a volume not usually used indoors. "My kids don't think I should be living alone. They want to put me in a home. They call it a 'community,' but it's a home. I thought if I could get married again to someone a little younger, I could stay in my house. I'm willing to fight my kids to leave you something for your trouble." He paused for a moment and looked at Jane appraisingly. "But you don't look desperate enough."

"You're right," Jane said. "I'm not."

"Thanks for your time." And with that, he rolled, very slowly, out of Phyllis's life. Behind the counter, the little barista stood, hands out, palms up, the universal symbol for "Whaddaya gonna do?"

Mark Pearson arrived at two forty-five. Although he seemed like an okay guy, his comb-over was so distracting, Jane barely heard a word he said. She found herself staring at it and daydreaming about its construction. It was pulled up and wound around in a structure that would have made Gustave Eiffel proud. Jane was not the least surprised to learn that Mr. Pearson was a civil engineer.

She felt terrible about crossing him off Phyllis's list for such a superficial reason. Perhaps he simply needed a kind person to whisper in his ear that the whole skyscraper needed to come down. But then, what did the comb-over say about his judgment if he thought he looked coffee-date ready with that thing on his head? What did it say about his self-confidence? After the whole Awful Craig crisis, Phyllis didn't need another project.

At three-fifteen, Guy Kroner, despite having checked on his Getadate profile "one or two glasses of wine a week" for alcohol and "never" for tobacco, reeked of alcohol and cigarettes. After he left, the girl behind the counter rolled her eyes. "Worst one yet," she sympathized.

By four o'clock, Jane was beginning to feel bad about having nothing positive to report to Phyllis. She'd had three cups of decaf and three trips to the restroom. The afternoon was turning into a bust.

And then, there he was. Harry Welch.

He was the only one who stood at the table, introduced himself properly, and shook Jane's hand. Jane was a sucker for that sort of thing, though in fairness, neither Calvin nor Guy could have probably stood for that long for any reason. When Harry took her hand, he shook it firmly and looked straight into her eyes with his own warm brown ones, which were framed by impressively bushy eyebrows. Although he had less hair now than he undoubtedly did at twenty, all he had appeared to be his own and it was worn on his head in the places nature intended.

Harry and Jane had both listed travel as an interest in their Getadate profiles, and he dove right into the topic. Where had she been on her last trip? He had covered the same territory and had been some places Jane never had—India, Australia, New

Zealand. They discovered they were both happy to travel alone but also enjoyed company. "Sometimes when my wife and I were traveling, we would split up during the day if we had different interests. It gives you even more to talk about at dinner."

Harry had been a widower for five years. With his sixty-sixth birthday approaching, he was "getting back out there" at the urging of his two grown sons, who both mercifully had homes of their own. Harry was a genial man, direct and curious, but the loss of his wife explained the sadness around his eyes. For the first time in decades, Jane felt something stirring. She had an impulse to make that sadness go away.

As the coffee date ended, Harry reached across the table and took Jane's hand. "I've enjoyed this a great deal. Can we perhaps consider dinner and a movie?"

Jane gave him her number. Then, her knees having turned to Jell-O like an adolescent's, she slid back down into her chair and watched him go. Behind the counter, the young barista raised her hands in the air and did a little victory dance.

"You want him for yourself," Helen said.

Jane had gone straight to Helen's house after she left Peet's. Helen's husband, Hugh, had been home reading the newspaper, but as soon as he'd seen the look on Jane's face, he'd hustled out. "Council of War," he said. "I'll leave you two."

Helen had poured two glasses of white wine. Jane had walked her through the afternoon, allegedly to validate the elimination of Calvin, Mark, and Guy as contenders. She wasn't sure what she intended to say about Harry. It turned out she didn't need to say much. As soon as Jane described him, Helen guessed.

"That's ridiculous," Jane responded. "I haven't been interested in a man in thirty years. Thirty-two, if you count the last two years with Francis."

"It's like riding a bicycle. You never forget."

"I haven't ridden a bicycle in thirty-two years, either, and I guarantee you are not going to see me zipping past your house anytime soon." When Helen said nothing, Jane continued. "You wouldn't be so eager, either, if the last time you were on a bike, riding along, happy and oblivious, a tractor trailer careened out of a side street, hit you, rolled over you, then backed up and rolled over you again." Jane stretched the metaphor beyond its breaking point.

"That's not quite the way it happened," Helen said. "Remember, I was there."

"Then I shouldn't have to tell you about it," Jane responded, a little testily.

Her former husband, Francis Darrowfield, had convinced her to renovate their kitchen to celebrate his getting tenure as an economics professor at Harvard. They had gutted it to the studs and sold all their old appliances. They had applied for, and Jane had cosigned, an enormous home equity loan.

Then Francis left.

After transferring the cash from the loan into a bank account only in his name.

And moved in with his department secretary.

Jane was left, humiliated, alone, in a home she couldn't afford, which had no kitchen. A judge eventually sorted it out, but it took forever, and more than once Jane thought she and Jonathan would be out on the streets.

Their friends chose sides. Jane got the bridge club. Francis got Harvard, and with Jane's marriage went her identity as a faculty wife. The only identity she'd had back then.

"I don't think the tractor trailer analogy is overstating," she said to Helen.

"That's not the part I object to. It was the part where you said you were riding along happy and oblivious. You were neither. You knew Francis didn't love you. You knew he would leave you someday. You were a nervous wreck, at least the last two years. You were willing to do anything to try to make him happy, including gutting a kitchen you loved. Including signing that loan. I've never been angry with Francis for leaving you, although the way he left was horrible. I've always been furious about what he did to you before he left. The way he made you feel about yourself."

Jane was silent for a moment. They'd never really talked about it quite this way. "I don't see what this has to do with my dilemma about Harry Welch," she finally said.

Helen drank the last of her wine. "I say go for it. If, and only if, you are ready to leave the past in the past."

"And you won't say anything to Phyllis?"

Helen held up three fingers on her right hand. "Scouts honor. It's between the two of you."

"I'll think about it," Jane answered.

"Good," Helen said. "How was your visit to Walden Spring?"

"Interesting. I got a tour of the buildings and then there was a food fight. Paul Peavey wants to me to move in."

"There was a what?"

"A food fight. That's the sort of community problem he wants me to help him address."

"Why would you need to move in to do that?"

"He wants me to experience the community in order to diagnose the problem."

Helen sat up even straighter. "The problem, I would think, is senior citizens flinging food around their dining room."

"That's the symptom, not the cause."

"I suppose. Will you do it?"

"Yes." Jane had not been certain until that moment, but now she was. "Yes, I will. I'll move in tomorrow."

Chapter Four

At eight-thirty the next morning, Jane called Paul Peavey and told him she was in. He sounded pleasantly surprised. She packed a suitcase; put together a canvas shopping bag full of staples; loaded her laptop, book, and assorted paraphernalia into another tote bag; and stopped the newspapers.

When she drove up, Walden Spring looked as serene as it had on the website. It was hard to imagine yesterday's melee had been real.

The guest unit turned out to be a Hawthorne. It was on the fourth floor in the first building, the one attached to the archway and Peavey's office. The balcony faced the quad—not the best view, but Jane could also see the golf course if she looked over the balcony's left side.

Regina Campbell led the way with the same chattering narrative as the day before. She gave Jane a keycard. "This will open your apartment, as well as your foyer downstairs and the other residential foyers. If you decide to buy, then you'd get one with your photo on it, which will be your Walden Spring ID card."

Jane walked her to the door. They stood in the hallway outside the apartment.

"Who else lives here?" Jane gestured to the three other doors that surrounded the elevator bank.

"Those units are empty," Regina answered. "Some of our last inventory. It's my job to sell them."

"Do the problems in the community make it difficult to sell the units?" Jane asked.

Regina's normally animated face went still. "I don't know what you're talking about." She left without saying good-bye.

Jane explored the apartment, examining the small appliances the real estate company had left there for the convenience of prospective buyers. She did the bits of unpacking she needed to do—clothes in the beautifully designed closet; coffee in the cupboard; milk, butter, and bread in the big, stainless steel refrigerator. At ten o'clock Jane went out on her balcony and looked at the green quadrangle below. Morning activities were about to begin. People scurried across the quad—or progressed at whatever pace their bodies allowed. She headed for the art room.

Evangeline opened the window in the art room as Jane arrived. The group in the room was even more heavily female than the day before. In fact, Maurice was the only man. "Such a lovely day," Evangeline announced. "Landscapes?"

The women all made positive noises, but Maurice sighed heavily. "Jeez, not again." They packed up their supplies and easels in a kind of kit and grabbed the folded campstools that were lined up along the wall.

"Welcome back, Jane," Evangeline said. She was dressed like a gypsy—colorful skirt, long silver earrings, headscarf. "I wasn't sure you'd return after yesterday."

"Glutton for punishment," Maurice mumbled.

Jane explained she was staying in the guest unit while she made her decision.

"Wonderful. Do you have your own art supplies? We have loaners." Evangeline fixed her up with a kit containing paints, palette, brushes, canvas, and a folding easel. Jane grabbed a campstool and lined up with the rest. Evangeline took her place in the front of the line.

"Where to?" one of the women asked.

"The fifth hole is stunning this time of day," Evangeline answered.

Evangeline led the way, walking swiftly on sure feet. The group stuck to the golf cart path. The terrain was hilly, and Jane wondered why Evangeline had picked a spot so far away. She slowed down and waited for a quite elderly lady as they climbed the last hill. Jane took the woman's campstool and artist kit and added them to her own.

"Thank you, dear," the old woman boomed. "I'm Ethel." She was tiny, with the most improbably deep bullfrog voice. Even allowing for age, she could never have been very big. Her voice had a unique quality, not the rasp of whiskey and cigarettes but the natural timbre of a much larger person.

"I'm Jane."

"Can you guess how old I am, Jane?"

At what age did people begin asking this question? There was only peril in the answer, whether one guessed too old or too young.

Fortunately, Ethel answered without waiting for Jane. "Ninety-one."

They came over the top of the rise, where the rest of the artists were setting up. "Well," Ethel said with satisfaction, "always a beautiful view."

It was, indeed, a gorgeous spot. The hill rolled down to an egg-shaped green. A charming bridge crossed a water hazard. Beyond that was a thin line of trees and then the fairway for another hole. A little cottage lay nestled, surrounded by bushes, on the far side of the fairway. The wet summer had worked its magic and everything was a different, brilliant shade of green.

But that wasn't the view the artists were focused on.

Below them, the grounds crew had arrived in a cart towing a ride-on mower. They were the same four who had broken up the food fight in the cafeteria the day before. They heaved themselves from the cart and went about their business, unloading the mower, grabbing edgers and hedge trimmers. Three of the four took off their shirts. The gasp from the artist group was audible.

"Hey, Karl," Evangeline yelled.

The fourth man waved back. "Hi, Mrs. Murray!" Then he too removed his shirt, turned around, and dropped it in the golf cart.

"My God." Jane hadn't meant to say it out loud. Karl was a magnificent specimen of a man. His body tapered from his broad shoulders through his strong back to his trim waist and well-muscled thighs. He bent over and picked something up off the ground.

Beside her, Ethel croaked happily. "A girl can dream, can't she?"

"Sheesh." Maurice had set up next to Evangeline. He was the only one who had any paint on his canvas. Despite the heat, he still had on his uniform of black blazer and black beret.

Jane placed her easel next to Evangeline on the other side.

"That's Karl Flagler," Evangeline explained. "He's the head groundskeeper. He poses for our life drawing classes sometimes in the winter."

By an hour later the grounds crew had moved on, and several foursomes had played the hole. Jane had been impressed by Karl and his crew. They were meticulous in their work, and though they joked and called out to one another, Karl let them know exactly what he wanted, and he got it from them.

By the time the crew left, most of the artists had managed to do some painting. Evangeline decreed that they'd stay another half an hour and then head back for lunch.

Jane pointed toward the bungalow across the way. "What's that?"

"Groundskeeper's cottage. Karl lives there."

"It looks old." The bungalow had weathered,

silver-gray shingles and lots of white gingerbread woodwork spidering along the roofline.

"It is. Walden Spring is built on the grounds of the old Wallingford estate. This golf course was private, part of the estate grounds. The groundskeeper's cottage is original."

"Where's the estate house?"

"Burned down in the 1970s. I lived less than a mile from here with my second husband then. Spectacular blaze. The old cellar hole has been filled in." Evangeline cocked her head toward a hill behind them, beyond the long-term care facility. "But there's still the remains of an enormous marble swimming pool, though most of the marble's been stolen over the years for local landscaping projects. I'll bet there are more marble walks and patios around here than any other town in Massachusetts."

Jane pointed in the other direction. "What's beyond the groundskeeper's cottage?"

"A line of trees. An older housing development. Then the town. If you look carefully you can see the steeple of the Trinitarian Congregational Church. Sometimes we cut through the trees to get to town. There are paths, but they're really only usable in the spring and fall when it's not icy or overgrown. Peavey doesn't like us doing it for safety reasons."

At that moment an older woman, accompanied by a caretaker, came walking along the path from the long-term care facility. The woman was well dressed in a summer skirt and top, and her long gray hair was carefully arranged in a bun. She was attractive, with large, wide-set eyes and a distinctive upturned nose. A Kevin Bacon nose. She walked over to Evangeline's canvas and admired it.

"Good morning, Mrs. Finnerty," Evangeline said.

The woman stared like she didn't have a clue who Evangeline was. She didn't even seem to respond to her own name, but some innate politeness asserted itself. "Have we met before?" she asked.

"Indeed," Evangeline said. "I live over in the condos. The same floor as Bill."

Mrs. Finnerty smiled broadly. "Oh, do you know my Billy?"

"I do."

"He's such a good boy."

"Yes," Evangeline answered. "He is."

Evangeline turned to Jane when they'd moved on. "Bill Finnerty's wife. Such a terrible disease."

"Terrible," Jane agreed. "She looks so much older than Bill."

"Yes, she does. Maybe it's the illness," Evangeline responded.

Eventually everyone did paint something. The route back to the clubhouse was long and hot. Jane again carried Ethel's things and fell behind the rest of the group as she slowed to keep pace with her. As they walked, Ethel blared in her foghorn voice about a beef with a long-dead sister-in-law. Jane made sympathetic noises.

By the time they got to the clubhouse, their fellow artists had put their kits away and gone off to lunch. The sounds of clattering cutlery and the smell of underseasoned food wafted into the art room from the dining hall below. Jane told Ethel to go directly to the dining room; she'd put their things away.

As Jane exited the art room, she saw Mike Witkowski leaving the game room next door. His leather jacket was off in a concession to the heat, and instead he wore a black T-shirt over black jeans. Although Jane guessed his age at late sixties or early seventies, his arms were sinewy, muscles visible. A strong old man. He held a wooden box— larger than a cigar box, smaller than a breadbox— under his left arm. He carefully closed the door to the game room, pulled on a fob hanging from his belt that held a bunch of keys, selected one, and locked the door. Locked it? Why was the game room locked with a key and not a keycard, like everything else in Walden Spring? And why did Mike Witkowski possess a key? It seemed more appropriate for a member of the staff.

Mike caught Jane watching him and gave a wag of his eyebrows, then hurried down the stairs to the cafeteria. She followed.

Chapter Five

Lunch passed without incident. The residents of Walden Spring were clumped into their respective cliques. Jane ate with the artists and dancers, keeping her ears tuned to their conversation, but her eyes glanced around the dining room observing the other groups.

The popular kids sat together, as before—the men in their golf clothes, the women in their bright summer shifts. One of those women stuck out from the crowd. Free of makeup and mousy haired, she wore a navy-blue tracksuit. Its dark color and total coverage made her look like a signet floating in a pond among a bunch of downy, yellow ducklings. What was her story?

Jane picked out some groups she hadn't noticed in the chaos of the day before. An obvious "couples" table. What happened when a spouse was lost? Did the survivor have to go sit elsewhere? Perhaps to one of the many tables that consisted only of women, or the much smaller number that had only men. One group at a table by a window was composed of the very old. Had they been at Walden Spring the longest—the senior seniors?

As lunch ended, Evangeline invited Jane for drinks on her balcony before dinner. "Apartment 325. Use your keycard to enter the foyer, then take the elevator up and knock on the door." Then she announced she was headed back to her apartment for a lie down. Maurice trailed her, though what role he might have in the lie down, if any, was still unclear to Jane.

Jane passed a pleasant afternoon on her balcony, observing the comings and goings of her fellow inmates. Groups headed to the tennis courts, rackets under their arms or over their shoulders, and returned later, walking more slowly, hair glistening with sweat. Golfers pulled their carts up to the tee closest to the condos and whacked at their balls. People walked, or rode their golf carts, toward the parking lot and returned later with grocery bags and packages. It was lovely and relaxing. If Jane hadn't witnessed the food fight, she would have wondered why Paul Peavey had hired her.

Her eyelids grew heavy. She was tempted to go for a lie down herself, but given the money Peavey was paying her, it didn't seem fair to do so.

At exactly four p.m., her cell phone rang, a Cambridge exchange.

"Jane? Harry Welch. How are you?"

"How nice to hear from you." Though he'd asked for her number at the end of their coffee date, Jane hadn't allowed herself to get her hopes up.

"How about a movie tomorrow night? I can pick you up at your house."

It was do-or-die time. Jane could turn him down and recommend her lovely friend Phyllis, or she could accept.

She hesitated so long, Harry cleared his throat and said, "I haven't asked a woman for a date in more than forty years. If I'm doing it wrong—"

"No, no, no," Jane rushed to reassure him. "You're doing it exactly right. I'd love to see a movie with you. What do you propose we should see?"

They picked a movie easily. No tussle over competing tastes, another positive sign. Harry confirmed the time, got her address, and rang off.

Jane didn't mention she wasn't at her house. That would require way too much explanation. Instead, she decided she would be at her house, to be picked up, by six o'clock the following evening.

Evangeline lived in one of the two-bedroom Alcott units. Her condo was colorfully and eclectically decorated, quite unlike the high-end hotel décor of the guest apartment where Jane was staying. The walls were crowded with Evangeline's canvases. Most were sweeping landscapes, though Karl Flagler was there, too, in the buff for all the world to see. Jane was as appreciative of the male form as the next person, though it was odd to see someone she had actually seen in real life. She was grateful Evangeline had warned her about the life drawing classes.

Maurice was the only other guest. Still in his black beret, he'd removed the blazer he'd worn over his black polo shirt. He and Evangeline were quite a pair. She sparkled with life, her purple ringlets shaking with every head nod. He sat slightly stooped, following her enthusiastic pronouncements with his more acerbic ones. They were obviously close, finishing each other's sentences, but Jane still couldn't tell—were they a couple or simply friends?

A cart opposite the windows in the living room was set up as an elaborate bar, complete with crystal ice bucket and bright chrome cocktail shaker. Jane accepted a white wine, feeling she was still "on duty." Evangeline and Maurice had Manhattans, which Evangeline concocted in what appeared to be a well-practiced ritual. Drinks in hand, they adjourned to the balcony, which, unlike Jane's, faced directly toward the golf course.

Evangeline passed hors d'oeuvres that consisted of a piece of processed cheese on a cracker with a slice of pimento-stuffed green olive on top. Maurice scarfed them down. Skinny as he was, he always seemed to be hungry.

Jane asked about the golf course.

"It was developed in the 1920s by the descendants of the owners of the mansion that was here," Evangeline said. "Much later, the family gave the house and land, including the golf course, to the town, and then decades later, the town sold it to the parent company that built Walden Spring. There was a terrific brouhaha about it, losing a public recreational facility like that, but it's a nice amenity for the community, and of course it looks lovely. Will you play while you're here?"

"I thought you couldn't get a tee time unless you were a friend of Bill Finnerty's," Jane said.

"Everyone says that," Evangeline said. "But there are ways around it. When my son-in-law visited in the spring, I baked Bill a plate of cookies. Bill gave him a perfect tee time in a wonderful foursome."

"Who put Bill in charge of the tee times?" Jane asked.

Maurice shrugged. "Peavey, I guess. Most courses would have a pro and a manager, but this little nine hole is just for the residents. Karl Flagler's in charge of the maintenance, and I guess they needed someone else to manage the playing times. Anyway, Finnerty's dictatorship shouldn't be allowed. The course is for the whole community."

"It must require a lot of upkeep," Jane said. "It's an expense all the residents bear. You should all be able to use it."

"Here, here." Maurice raised a glass to Jane.

"Do you play?" Jane asked.

"Can't stand it," Maurice answered.

"Powder room?" Jane asked Evangeline.

"Use the one off my bedroom," she said, pointing back into the unit and down the hall.

Evangeline's bedroom and bath were as stylish and eccentric as the rest of the apartment. The walls were painted a pleasant, neutral color and lined with her canvases. The fabric—bedspread, curtains, table scarves—were in bold reds, yellows, and greens. As in the rest of the apartment, there were no personal photos of travel destinations, husbands, or kids. Crowded out by her artwork, Jane supposed. She stopped to admire a set of three paintings over the bed. Unlike the sweeping landscapes in the rest of the unit, these were precise, close-up oil studies of a wall, crumbling concrete shot through with deep crevices with bits of marble clinging to the rough surface here and there. Jane had to give it to Evangeline. She was good. Jane felt if she touched a painting, her fingertips would feel the rough surface of the stone.

When she returned to the balcony, Evangeline and Maurice had refreshed their cocktails and Jane's wineglass had been topped off.

Jane had hardly sat back down on the rattan love seat when there was a terrific noise from the parking lot. Mike Witkowski and his motorcycle gang roared into the quad, shattering the quiet of the late afternoon. They stopped their bikes under the column of balconies kitty-corner from Evangeline's and revved the engines, making a horrible racket. Doris Milner came out on a second-story balcony and yelled at the riders to pipe down. Her threats were met by catcalls and general hilarity from Mike's group.

"Jeez, this again." Maurice pulled his cell phone from the pocket of his slacks and pushed some buttons.

Bill Finnerty, face red with anger, appeared behind Doris on her balcony. "Cut out the noise!" he shouted. "Or, I'll—"

"You'll what?" Mike called back. "You'll go to Peavey? Ha!"

"We'll call the cops!" Doris screamed. "The hell with Peavey. We're reporting you for disturbing the peace."

"I don't think so," Mike called back. "Bill doesn't want the cops involved any more than I do, right, Bill?"

"Too late!" Maurice shouted from Evangeline's balcony, cell phone at his ear. "I already called. They're on their way."

Then things happened quickly. As Paul Peavey made his way from his office under the archway three of Bill's plaid-pants golfing buddies dashed onto Doris's balcony and heaved water balloons onto the gang below. The first balloon caught Paul on the side of his head and soaked him. The next one flooded Leon's sidecar. While Mike's gang cursed and turned their bikes around, Mike stood his ground, staring up at Bill. "Watch your back!" he called. "I'll get you."

Maurice shook his head. "How old are these guys?"

"Old enough to know better," Evangeline answered, disgusted.

The evening seemed to be at an end.

"Might as well head to the dining room. I'm sorry," Evangeline apologized. "We'll try this again sometime when there isn't a free-for-all going on."

Chapter Six

Dinner was indeed served at the tables, though the food itself was even less inspiring than lunch. The dull palate of skinless chicken; brown rice; and watery, overcooked broccoli looked nothing like the colorful photos on the website.

Paul made the rounds of the tables. He'd changed out of his water-soaked suit into another, complete with tie, which seemed an odd thing to wear so late in the day. It was as if he needed the suit to use as armor, to create the proper distance between him and the variously dressed, but definitely unsuited, residents.

The people of Walden Spring obviously liked Paul. Although they complained about the motorcycles and the water balloons, they also chatted with him easily about hobbies and grandchildren and made small requests about things like loose screens and squeaky doors. Jane thought he took a genuine interest in the residents, a strong sense of mission in his work of making Walden Spring a great place to live. Jane was glad she'd signed on to help him.

It was all very pleasant until he got to the artists' table.

"Jeez, Paul, you gotta make this stop," Maurice complained. "I was enjoying a lovely cocktail when those cycles started roaring. I coulda had a coronary."

"I'm sorry. We're working on it." Paul looked so conspiratorially at Jane, she was worried the others would guess why she was there. But the conversation moved on.

When Paul left the clubhouse, Jane pushed her plate away and excused herself. She caught up with him in the quad.

"What's the prognosis?" he asked as they strolled toward his office.

"I can see why you hired me."

"Any ideas yet?"

"Yes," Jane answered, "two. Why does Mike have a key to the game room? Why does it even have that kind of lock? The other doors in Walden Spring use a keycard."

Paul stopped walking and considered. "There's a lot of expensive equipment in there. Flat-screen TVs and gaming equipment. Mike came to me, we talked, and I agreed it was better to keep it locked when the room wasn't in use. He wanted an old-fashioned lock, not a card reader, so I had one installed and gave him the key. He seemed like the logical person, since he uses the room so much."

"You need to take the key away from Mike." Jane said it firmly.

"Sure," Paul agreed immediately. "But why?"

"Cliques thrive on territoriality and exclusivity." They started walking again. "Mike's taken over the game room as his group's private domain. The other residents feel they can't use it. By giving Mike the key, Walden Spring is officially sanctioning that behavior. You're not just saying it's okay, you're enabling it. The message from you as executive director has to be that exclusive use of community property isn't tolerated."

"Okay. I get it. I'll speak to him. You said you had two ideas."

"At the same time, you have to take assigning tee times away from Bill Finnerty."

"What! Why?" Paul stopped again.

"Same reason. Just as the game room doesn't belong to Mike and his guys, the golf course doesn't belong to Bill's crew."

"But you have to admit, both the dustups you've seen—the food fight on your first visit and the water balloon fight tonight—were started by Mike."

"The residents feel just as oppressed by Bill as they do by Mike." Jane outlined the abuses of power she'd heard about—the bribe of cookies Bill had extracted from Evangeline and the man who hadn't been able to get a tee time all summer.

"That's terrible," Paul agreed. "I wish people would come to me with this sort of thing. But maybe—just throwing out ideas here—maybe I should take the key from Mike and wait awhile, see if that helps, before I move on to Bill."

Why was Paul so much more reluctant to confront Bill than Mike? On the surface, Mike was much more intimidating. "That's exactly what you shouldn't do," Jane responded. "You're not taking Bill's side or Mike's side. You're laying out standards for the public space in the community and applying them equally."

"Okay." Paul sighed. "I'll talk to them both tonight."

"What have I gotten you into?" Irma wondered aloud after Jane described the water balloon fight.

"Don't apologize." Jane adjusted her cell phone, bringing it closer to her ear. "It's been really interesting."

"Have you figured it all out?"

"Some of it, I hope."

Irma was the newcomer to the bridge group. Thirty-two years earlier, Helen proposed Irma as a replacement for a woman Jane barely remembered, who'd moved somewhere. Cleveland? Cincinnati? Columbus? Phyllis and Jane had been resistant, even suspicious. The three of them were young married mothers then. Irma was "other." Older, unmarried. Jane's great-aunt would have called her a "maiden lady." And then there was Irma's house. Sharing an apartment with her mother, renting out the lower floor, on the wrong side of Huron Avenue. Outside Harvard's orbit.

Helen, who'd met Irma through Hugh's work at Mount Auburn Hospital, had insisted. Irma loved bridge. Irma was a hoot. They needed a fourth. At least give her a try.

Now Jane was deeply embarrassed by her naïve snobbism. Were their lives really so insular back then? Products of the civil rights generation, they

would have bristled at the idea of shunning someone who was of a different race or religion. But the
smallest difference of class, of education, of neighborhood, had made her a coward. In the years
since, at the phone company in all its incarna-
tions, Jane had worked with people from every
conceivable background, who led every conceivable kind of life. But thirty years ago, she'd been
struggling behind closed doors, married to a man
who no longer loved her, raising a difficult child,
and trying to keep up the fiction, to herself and all
around her, that everything was fine.

Irma, it turned out, was widely read and terribly
funny. Although she'd never married, she was neither a virgin nor a prude. She was the most gener-
ous person Jane knew in every sense of the word
and a great friend.

"I called to ask about Evangeline and Maurice,"
Jane said. "I had cocktails with them tonight."

"Ah, Evangeline." Irma chuckled. "We met at
work. She was an art therapist. She was passionate
about the job. You'll find she's passionate about
everything."

"What happened to her husband?"

"Husbandzzz." Irma emphasized the "s." "There
were four. Divorced. Died. Divorced. Died."

"Beheaded. Lived," Jane responded.

"Not quite in Henry the Eighth's league." Irma
laughed.

"But a goodly number. Does she have kids?"

"Yes. Two from marriage one, and two from marriage three. They're all grown. Spread around the
country. I get the sense they're not around much."

"Hum."

"Hum, what?"

Hum, the distance adult children kept was dangerous ground for Jane. "What's the deal with Maurice?" she asked.

"I've never quite figured it out. He's been hanging around her for the past couple of years. I think Evangeline loves him, in the sense that you'd love a particularly devoted dog."

"Thanks," Jane said. "That's helpful. Best to Minnie."

"You're welcome." Irma sounded relieved. "I'm just glad you're not mad."

Jane watched TV on the enormous flat screen mounted over the gas fireplace, then turned in. But sleep didn't come. A strange bed in a strange place was seldom welcoming. And, despite how sure she'd sounded, Jane was nervous about the advice she'd given Paul. Had she been precipitous—too anxious to prove her value? Should she have assessed more before she recommended?

She tossed. And turned. She got up and went to the bathroom. She returned to bed and read a little. She stared at the clear surfaces of the bedroom in the guest apartment, beautifully decorated but so impersonal. She turned out the bedside light. Then tossed and turned and repeated the whole sequence. At a little before one a.m. she gave up, got out of bed, and headed to the living room.

Jane opened the slider and walked onto the balcony. The heat hit her like a warm, wet towel. The day hadn't cooled when the sun went down. If anything it had gotten more humid. Around her, almost all the condo windows were dark, as was the clubhouse. Some lights shone from the long-term care facility in the distance, but it, too, slumbered. The waning moon was a sliver in the night sky, throwing no light, but in front of her the quad was well lit with faux gas, cast-iron street lamps along the paths.

Wait. What was that? Jane barely caught the movement along the periphery of the lawn. A person. Staying off the well-lit paths. Moving swiftly, confidently. Although she couldn't see clearly, she was sure it was a man. Wearing dark clothing. Tall. Headed for the golf course.

She stared, fascinated, as the man walked to the edge of the golf course and started across. He disappeared into the darkness. What a strange thing to do. Walk around on a golf course in the middle of the night.

Chapter Seven

Wednesday, August 8

At last, Jane fell into a deep but all too short sleep. As a city dweller she was used to the rumble of trash barrels being wheeled toward the curb and the slamming of car doors at all hours. But just past dawn there was such a hubbub outside her window, she couldn't ignore it. Brakes screeched, people shouted, and feet pounded, running across asphalt. Jane got up; put on her long, light-blue bathrobe; and peered over her balcony. Half a dozen police cars were pulled up by Peavey's office. Clumps of official-looking people stood on the edge of the golf course.

Jane dressed hastily. By the time she got outside, most of Walden Spring was gathered around the quad, talking in low voices. She spotted Evangeline's purple ringlets in the crowd.

"What's happened?" Jane asked when she reached her.

"A dead body. On the golf course." Evangeline's voice quavered. Her eyes were wet with tears that threatened to escape down her cheeks. She was clearly freaked out.

"Good heavens." Even though she'd assumed the worst when she saw the number of police cars, Jane was shocked.

"Out on the seventh hole. They say Karl Flagler found it," someone in the crowd said.

"Probably a homeless person sleeping outside who died out there," someone else speculated.

"Because there are so many homeless people in Concord," Maurice responded.

"Could be someone from long-term care, wandered away," a man near them guessed.

"Or a kid from town. Drugs," another suggested.

Jane thought about the figure she'd seen walking out onto the golf course. Could the body be his?

A black medical examiner's van pulled up to the edge of the parking lot. A man got out of the passenger side. A plainclothes cop went up to talk to him.

"Anybody read lips?" someone called out. Escorted by the officers, the medical examiner started across the golf course in the direction of the seventh hole.

A uniformed cop came over and called to the group. "Go on about your business. We'll be talking to each of you later."

Nobody moved. Of course, almost nobody in this crowd had a business to go to. The cop, oblivious, repeated himself. People grumbled and scuffled their feet.

"Okay, let's eat," Maurice said.

"Eat!" Evangeline looked horrified.

Maurice shrugged. "If I gave up eating every time someone around here croaked, I'd be even skinnier than I am."

Breakfast was sparsely attended, the conversation subdued. Then a thrum of raised voices began at one end, rippling across the dining room like a tide. "It's Bill Finnerty," someone at the next table said. "The body on the golf course. Beat to death with his own club."

Evangeline was barely keeping it together. Her hand shook as she brought a forkful of scrambled eggs to her lips. One of the other artists put an arm around her and said, "How awful to think something like that happened here."

Maurice shook his head and shoveled more bran flakes into his mouth.

Jane understood Evangeline's shock, because she felt it herself. She and Bill Finnerty hadn't exchanged a single word, but she'd observed him and passed judgment on him. And last night, she'd told Paul to remove the source of Bill's power in the community, the scheduling of the tee times. Jane snuck a peek at Bill and Doris's usual table. Deserted.

"But who would beat Bill to death?" one of the dancers asked.

"Isn't it obvious?" Maurice looked pointedly at

Mike Witkowski's table. Mike sat, elbows on the table, hands folded in front of his face, deep in thought.

"Do you really think Mike would kill Bill?" Jane asked, worried she'd played some unwitting part in it. What if Mike was so angry when Paul took the game room key away, he'd killed his enemy? But that made no sense.

"Of course not!" the little dancer exclaimed.

Maurice shrugged. "Okay then, think Doris did it?" This set off another wave of chatter around the table.

"Why would Doris murder Bill?" Jane asked.

Silence. Then Maurice said, "Let's just say she wasn't the only hen in Bill's chicken coop."

"Maurice," Evangeline scolded. "The man is *dead*."

"I'm just saying if it wasn't Mike, maybe Doris had finally had enough."

This drove the table deep into discussion about that possibility. Then, as quickly as the conversation had surged, it quieted. A uniformed policeman came through the crowd, walked up to the table, and stood across from Jane.

"Mrs. Darrowfield?"

Jane nodded.

"You're wanted in Mr. Peavey's office."

All eyes in the dining room were trained on her as she followed the policeman out.

Paul's outer office was crowded with cops: uniformed Concord cops, plainclothes cops, state cops, cops of every size and description. And the most surprising cop of all, Detective Tony Alvarez, the baby-faced detective from the Cambridge Police Department Fraud Squad. The one who had thought Jane was ninety-six-year-old Minnie Brittleson.

Despite the change in her hair color since the last time she'd seen him, he gave Jane a nod of recognition when he spotted her, though he said nothing, so neither did Jane. She wondered what he could possibly be doing fifteen miles out of the jurisdiction of his force, at a Concord homicide.

Paul Peavey opened the door of the inner office. "Ah, Jane, you're here. Come in."

There were more plainclothes cops in Peavey's office. A man well into his fifties, with a bald head surrounded by a fringe of salt-and-pepper hair, was obviously in charge. He introduced himself as Detective Fitz of the Massachusetts State Police.

They all looked at Peavey, who hesitated for a long, uncomfortable moment before he spoke. "Jane, we called you because, naturally, with all the things we've had going on in the community, you know, our little 'problems,' I assumed, well, and since ours is a private golf course, the police assumed . . . that maybe it was someone in the community, who, you know, with all the 'hostility,' but now we have new information, and it appears we may be dealing with something else entirely." He breathed out noisily when he finished speaking.

Jane had trouble following Paul's speech from the first, and by the end found it practically incomprehensible. "Is the body Bill Finnerty?" she asked, in an attempt to clarify. "That's the story that's going around."

Paul glanced at the senior detective, who gave a

slight head nod. "It would appear so," Peavey answered cautiously.

"And was it murder?"

This time Detective Fitz answered. "Yes."

Jane considered. "What you have just told me is that you originally thought the murder might have had something to do with the reason you hired me, but in the time it took for the trooper to locate and retrieve me, your assessment changed."

"We are in possession of some new information," the older detective confirmed.

Jane felt a great weight lift from her shoulders. The police didn't think the motive had anything to do with the advice she'd given Peavey. It didn't have anything to do with her assignment at Walden Spring at all.

"When is the last time you saw the victim?" Detective Fitz looked at Jane.

"Last night at dinner," she said.

"The same as Mr. Peavey," Detective Fitz said.

Paul furrowed his brow. "Yes," he answered, "last night at dinner."

So Paul hadn't spoken to Bill about the tee times, as Jane had recommended and as he had promised. She tried to catch his eye, but he was looking everywhere except at her.

"Sorry to have brought you in here unnecessarily, Jane," Peavey said.

"I'm glad it was unnecessary," Jane answered honestly. "I assume you'll want to terminate my assignment and send me home?" She hadn't wanted to ask him about her work in front of the assembled cops, but she reckoned he'd be tied up with them for quite a while.

Paul paled. "What? Why would you think that? The community will be more unsettled than ever."

Although Jane didn't disagree with his assessment, she wasn't the kind of professional he needed. Grief counselors would be more like it. But it wasn't the time to argue with Paul. She'd wait until she could speak to him privately.

"We'd prefer you didn't leave right away," Detective Fitz said. "We'll be around to interview all the residents. I can't make you stay, but we'll make a special effort to get to you today."

"Thank you. I'll certainly stay for that." She had, after all, to tell them about the dark figure that had walked across the golf course. Now that it had been established the victim was Bill Finnerty, had she seen the perpetrator? She said her good-byes, smiling at Detective Alvarez as she passed back through the crowded reception room. He smiled back.

Chapter Eight

It was ten o'clock by the time Jane returned to her unit. When she opened her door, her phone buzzed away on the granite kitchen countertop. She couldn't reach it in time to answer, so she checked her recent calls. Ten from Helen, seven from Phyllis, four from Irma.

She called Helen back.

"Jane, thank goodness you're all right. We thought you'd been murdered. It's all over the news."

"You don't watch the news in the morning." Jane knew Helen's habits as well as she knew her own. Morning news in the Graham household consisted of the *Boston Globe* and the *New York Times*, both in print editions. The TV wouldn't be turned on before the local news at six.

"Phyllis called almost hysterical and said to turn on the TV right away," Helen said. "We knew you were getting yourself into something, taking this job, but murder! We never imagined."

"Neither did I. In any case, the victim is a man. His body was found this morning on the golf course."

"So you'll be coming home now." It wasn't a question. It was a conclusion, almost a demand.

"Not right away." Jane settled on the barstool in front of the counter. "I still have to be interviewed by the police."

"The police? Why?"

"It's nothing. Standard. They're interviewing all the residents."

"Then you'll come home?"

"We'll see." Jane changed the subject, throwing out a shiny object she knew Helen couldn't resist. "Harry Welch asked me on a date."

"When? Where?"

"You don't need to sound so surprised. Tonight. He's picking me up at my house."

"You've made your decision. You're keeping him for yourself." Was there a hint of condemnation in Helen's voice? Or perhaps Jane's guilty conscience heard it there.

"Will you call Phyllis and Irma and let them know I'm okay? But please, don't say anything to Phyllis about Harry. I'll find my own way to tell her."

It was one little date. Who knew, they might hate each other by the time it was over. Maybe he was one of those people who talked through the whole movie, or slurped his drink, or picked popcorn out of his teeth. It was more than likely things would end before they began. Probably, there would be no need to tell Phyllis.

"Of course not. That's between the two of you.

At least this date with Harry means you'll be home by tonight."

"Maybe, though I might come back here afterward. I've only talked briefly to the man who hired me, but he wants me to stay and continue with my assignment."

"And what was your assignment?"

"To cut down the level of hostility in the community."

"Well," Helen said, "great job so far."

Jane showered, re-dressed, and tried to keep busy, but there wasn't much to do in the bare-bones apartment. When the police still hadn't contacted her about an interview by eleven o'clock, she slathered on sunblock, grabbed a baseball cap, and set out for a walk.

The commotion in the quad and parking lot had wound down. The medical examiner's van was gone, along with some of the police cars, though several were still clustered up by Peavey's office, along with a police van and three news station satellite trucks. Jane checked to see if one of the cars was marked CAMBRIDGE PD, but no go.

She wandered along the same golf cart path she'd taken with the artists the day before, turning the events of the last twenty-four hours over in her mind. She'd accepted a consulting job and moved to Walden Spring. She'd witnessed a food fight and a water balloon fight, and she'd heard Mike Witkowski taunt Bill Finnerty about not wanting to attract the attention of the police. She'd recommended to Paul Peavey that he remove a source of power from Bill and one from Mike, though based on what Paul had told the state police, he hadn't spoken to Bill after dinner. Had he talked to Mike? Paul had seemed much more open to speaking to Mike. Why was that? Finally, she'd seen a figure dressed in black walk onto the golf course at one in the morning. A golf course where a murder had occurred.

The spot where they'd painted had a good view of the area across the fifth to the seventh hole, where the body had been found. Jane crested the small hill and was surprised to see Karl Flagler sitting on a rock outcropping, staring dejectedly at the scene. She thought perhaps she should leave him alone, but he turned and saw her.

"They won't let me go back to my place." He stared out across the golf course, back slumped, voice dejected. Jane followed his gaze to the site where the body must have been about fifty yards from his cottage. The corpse was gone, but people in plastic jumpsuits still combed through the grass on the green, searching for something. Uniformed police officers walked through the line of trees on the other side of the course. A golf cart stood on the path not far from the body site.

Jane sat down a few feet away from Karl on the same boulder. He was tanned and well-muscled from working outdoors, as handsome up close as he had been from a distance. Jane put his age somewhere in his midthirties. He had a strong chin and a Roman nose. He looked even better than he did in Evangeline's painting, like a statue come to life.

"I heard you found the body. That must have

been hard." She turned to face him. "Jane Darrow-field. Call me Jane."

He looked at her. "Karl Flagler. Karl. I know who you are. Or, why you're here, I should say."

So much for Paul keeping her assignment confidential. "I know who you are, too. I assume the police have already interviewed you."

"Yup." He gave her a small smile. "Next time I find a body I'm going to keep walking."

"That tough, huh? Do you mind if I ask you what happened?"

Karl shrugged his muscular shoulders. "Not much to tell. I got up just as the sun was rising. I'm always up early in the summer when we're the busiest. I noticed the golf cart out on the course right away. I recognized it as Bill's. I didn't think much about it. Sometimes the kids from the town come over here at night and steal the carts and drive them around. I was annoyed I had to deal with it. I walked a little ways onto the course, and there he was, on the ground, the back of his head . . ." Karl couldn't go on.

"The rumor is he was killed with a golf club."

"Seems possible. I didn't see a club near the body. He looked pretty well beaten. His bag was in his cart. I didn't stop to count his clubs or anything. Just called the cops." Karl took something from his pocket and worried it in his strong hands. Jane caught a glimpse of it—a man's wedding ring, though there was no tan line on Karl's ring finger.

"Do you live alone?" she asked.

He seemed surprised by the question, until he saw her looking at his moving hands. "Oh, this." He balanced the gold ring on his palm. "It was my father's. I carry it for luck. I live alone. The cottage comes with the job and it's too good a perk to pass up, even though it means—"

"Living surrounded by old people?"

He laughed, and the corners of his eyes showed little lines caused by working in the sun that made him even more attractive. "Something like that." He looked across the lush golf course toward the line of trees on the other side. "The truth is, I love it here. It's beautiful. In the spring when everything's blooming. In the fall when the leaves are so bright."

"Like Heaven's waiting room?"

He laughed again. "You know a better place?"

Jane liked this man, who cared about Walden Spring and who was a good boss, obviously skilled at his job. "Your story sounds pretty straightforward. Why are the police giving you a hard time?"

"Dunno. Maybe because I found the body. Or maybe because everybody here knew I hated that creep, Bill Finnerty."

Jane was deeply curious about why Karl had hated Bill, but when he didn't say more she decided not to press him in a moment when he was obviously stretched thin emotionally. She sat with him in what she hoped was comforting silence for a few minutes and then said her good-byes.

Suddenly, it was time for lunch. Lifecare communities were like cruise ships. They were constantly bulk feeding you. People poured into the quad. Jane followed the crowd.

But when she joined the artists and dancers in

line, she saw that the lunch choices were paltry. "Please, sir, I want some more." Maurice grimaced as he accepted a bowl of chicken noodle soup.

"Don't blame me," the large woman behind the counter said. "I expected both my meat and produce trucks this morning. The police won't let them in."

Maurice looked around. "Oh, dear. If this keeps up we'll have to resort to eating one another. Which will be hard on some, given the toughness of our meat and the looseness of our dentures."

"Shut it, Maurice," Mike Witkowski commanded from ahead of him in line. Maurice shut it.

Evangeline was absent from lunch. Jane wasn't surprised. She'd barely eaten breakfast. Apparently, the need the rest of them felt to be together and trade news didn't sit so well with her sensitive, artistic soul. At the table, they got down to the serious business of comparing notes. Several people had already been interviewed by the state police detectives.

"I told the detective who interviewed me something," one of the dancers said. They all leaned in. "Last night, I had to drive to town to pick up some antacid. As I passed Paul Peavey's office on my way to the parking lot"—she paused dramatically—"all the windows were open"—another pause—"and Paul was having an argument with lots of yelling with"—third pause—"Bill Finnerty."

There were gasps all around.

This was different, and in direct contradiction to what Peavey had told Detective Fitz. "What were they fighting about?" Jane was afraid she knew, but she had to ask.

"I don't know." The dancer was indignant. "I'm not an eavesdropper. And I had no way to know Bill would be dead by this morning."

"What did the detective say about it when you told him?" Jane pressed.

"He was *very* interested, I can tell you. Asked me tons of questions. Was I sure it was Bill? Was I sure it was Paul? What time was the fight? Do I wear hearing aids?"

"What time was this fight?" Jane kept pushing.

"It was around seven-thirty, a bit before sunset. I was rushing because I don't like to drive after dark."

So, Paul must have spoken to Bill Finnerty about the tee times after dinner. Why did he lie about it to the cops?

"What do *you* know?" Maurice demanded, staring at Jane. "Why did the police come looking for you at breakfast?"

What could she tell them? Certainly not why she was there or the advice she'd given Paul. "Oh, that. I saw someone walking on the golf course last night."

"You saw the killer!" the dancer said.

"I don't know who I saw," Jane clarified.

"You saw the ghost!" It was Ethel, the little woman whose art supplies Jane had carried, her deep voice booming. "The ghost killed Bill." Her eyes were bright with more merry excitement than you might expect for someone talking about murder and the paranormal.

"*Blurg.*" Maurice coughed into his soup.

Jane ignored him. "The ghost?"

Ethel was so tiny, Jane could barely see her over

her bowl of soup, but she told the story in her giant, rasping voice. "Walden Spring has two ghosts. The first is the beautiful Susannah. She came here to the Wallingford estate as the naïve second wife of George Wallingford, the owner. She never could fit in and the staff was in mourning for his first wife who he built the mansion for. They gave Susannah a terrible time. She fell in love with the gamekeeper, who lived in the cottage where Karl lives now. He brought out something in her she had never felt before. She became pregnant and was going to run away with him, but her husband locked her in the attic."

"How awful." Jane played along.

Ethel was deadly serious. "That's not the worst of it. Then the estate burned down. The firemen tried to rescue her, but she was dancing on the parapet and fell to her death."

"Terrible," Jane sympathized, not mentioning that they'd just been given a fast walk through *Rebecca* and *Lady Chatterley's Lover* with a little *Jane Eyre* thrown in for good measure. Or that, according to Evangeline, the mansion had burned down in the early 1970s.

"That's not all. After he heard Susannah died with their baby, the gamekeeper hung himself in the cottage." Ethel paused for dramatic effect. "Now they both walk these grounds searching for each other."

Half the people at the table were looking away, embarrassed, but the other half were rapt. "Why would the ghost kill Bill?" Jane asked, in spite of her better instincts.

"Couldn't get a tee time," Maurice grumped.

Chapter Nine

It was a long, hot walk back through the quad. The sun was high in the sky. Jane almost reached the entrance door to the foyer for her building when Regina Campbell, the in-house realtor, came fast-walking down the path. Her brown hair was pulled back in a ponytail, and she was dressed in Lycra shorts and a black sports bra. Jane had seen Regina wear only her realtor power suit, and she looked very different in athletic gear. She was fit, no question about that, broad and muscled through the shoulders and tall even without her high heels.

"Going for a run?" Jane asked.

"Yeah, I usually run early in the morning, before it gets so hot, but this morning . . ." She let the sentence dangle, as if she didn't want to finish it. "I feel lousy if I don't run every day. Works out my frustrations."

Regina kept walking and Jane fell in step beside her, which was not easy, because Regina's strides were much longer than Jane's. "Your frustrations?" Jane prompted

"Well, it was hard enough to sell these units before the murder, what with the motorcycle gang, the food fights, but now—it's going to be impossible. I figure it's just a matter of time before they fire me." Regina slowed down a bit so Jane could catch up. "With you, I thought maybe I had a live one, but I know you're not here to buy a unit. Karl told me."

Good grief. Did everybody know why Jane was there, or only the employees? Was Regina's voice just a tad proprietary when she said the name "Karl"?

"I'm sorry about that. Paul thought it was best if no one knew about my assignment."

"Paul. Bah. What a baby. Why didn't he just man up and take care of things himself instead of hiding behind you? I'll never understand why Paul couldn't stand up to Bill. What did that guy have on him?" Regina strode on, apparently unaware that she'd just given Paul a perfect motive for murder. Jane cantered to keep pace with her.

Even though Jane liked Paul, she also had thought Paul was unnaturally reluctant to confront Bill. Much more reluctant than to confront Mike, who was outwardly the tougher customer. *Did* Bill Finnerty have something on Paul?

Jane turned back to Regina. "It's amazing you've lasted as long as you have. If you couldn't sell units, why didn't you quit?"

"I tried to quit, but Paul begged me to stay. I don't think he wanted to have to tell the higher-ups in the big corporation that owns this place that the situation here was so dire no realtor would represent it. So he offered me an apartment rent free to keep me. I live in a Hawthorne unit. That keeps my expenses to a minimum. With the housing prices around here, I haven't been motivated to quit."

This was news. "I didn't realize you lived here."

"Oh, yeah. It's a party and a half. Now the corporate owners of Walden Spring have got to know they won't sell anything for a while, so they'll make me go anyway."

Detective Fitz arrived at Jane's apartment to interview her in the late afternoon. She invited him in. Fitz immediately sat on the end of the couch she had claimed as her own. How a person could have a "spot" in an apartment where she'd stayed all of twenty-four hours was one of the mysteries of the human condition. But Jane did, and Fitz was in it.

"Do you mind if I sit there?" Jane pointed to her book and glasses on the end table next to Fitz.

"I'll stay here, if you don't mind," Fitz responded.

Jane did mind but saw no value in fighting further. She moved to one of the high-backed living room chairs that faced the couch. Fitz got right to business, explaining that the Concord police didn't investigate murders and the Massachusetts State Police were handling the investigation. Fitz rushed through a series of routine questions, sounding bored, as if he had been asking the residents of Walden Spring the same questions all day, which he almost surely had.

"Where were you between the hours of midnight and five a.m.?" he asked.

Interesting question, Jane thought. That must have been when the murder occurred. "Here in the apartment and, briefly, outside on the balcony."

That brought him up short. "You were on your balcony between midnight and five?"

"For a little while, yes. I couldn't sleep and thought fresh air would do me good."

Fitz wrote something in his notebook. "Did you see or hear anything out of the ordinary?"

"It was my first night in Walden Spring. I don't know what is ordinary. I did see a man, dressed in black, who came from the condo complex and walked across the golf course at one o'clock or so."

Now she had his full attention. "Did you recognize this person?"

"No."

"Could it have been the victim?"

"The figure I saw was tall, much taller than Finnerty. And Bill had a distinctive way of walking—a puffed-out, cock-on-the-walk type of posture. The man I saw didn't move like that."

"How did you know the man you saw was tall?"

How had she formed that impression? "When he cut across the drive between the quad and the golf course, he passed by a street lamp. He was tall relative to the lamppost."

Detective Fitz sat forward on the couch. "Did you see this person in the light? Do you remember anything distinguishing about him? Hair color? Skin color? Anything."

"He was dressed in black. His back was to me. I'm sorry."

"Did you wear your spectacles when you went out on the balcony?" Fitz looked pointedly at her glasses beside him on the end table.

"I wear glasses only for reading. My vision is otherwise excellent."

"Even at night?"

"Yes, at night. I'm usually the designated driver in my group of friends." Jane stopped, thinking perhaps she'd painted the bridge group as hard partiers, which was not at all the case. Jane drove because she liked to drive.

"And your memory? Do you ever have trouble remembering things, how they happened, when they happened?"

"Absolutely not!" That wasn't true, strictly speaking. Jane sometimes entered a room and had no idea why she'd gone there or had to hunt high and low for her car keys. But that was normal, right? "I couldn't be mistaken about the night I saw the man, because I've been here only one night," she said, rather testily. Who was Fitz to ask her these questions, anyway? The black curls that surrounded his baldpate were shot through with white hairs, and his body had gone soft. He was on her side of fifty for certain.

"Got it. How did the figure move? Was he running, walking, strolling?"

"Walking quickly. Lithely."

"No limp or other impediment?"

"He wasn't infirm, if that's what you're asking."

"Why did you think he'd come from one of the condos here?"

Jane took her time to answer. "Because I first

spotted him in the quad. I couldn't say for sure, though."

Fitz looked her full in the face. She had a sense the next question was important. "You're certain it was a man?"

Was she? There was something about the figure's height, shape, movement that said male. But then Jane remembered Regina Campbell barreling down the path in the quad. Jane pictured her—tall and broad-shouldered, hair pulled back. "I definitely thought it was a man at the time, but now that you ask, I can't be absolutely certain."

Fitz made a note, then looked back at her. "Is there more you'd like to tell me about the figure you saw, or anything else?"

Jane hesitated. The little dancer had already told the police she'd heard Paul and Bill arguing in Paul's office after dinner. "When you called me into Paul's office this morning, I assume he had told you what I'm doing here at Walden Spring."

Detective Fitz drew his salt-and-pepper eyebrows together. "He did. And I must say I had quite a negative reaction to the idea of bringing an un-trained civilian into a situation that had already re-sulted in multiple calls to the Concord Police Department."

"Paul didn't ask me to jump into the scrum," Jane reassured him. "He wanted my insights into the causes of the problems and suggestions on how to solve them." She shifted uneasily in the un-familiar chair. "You might have heard Bill Finnerty was in charge of the tee times on the golf course." Jane waited until Fitz gave a slight nod. "He used that job unfairly and to his advantage. Yesterday, immediately after dinner, I advised Paul to end Finnerty's power to schedule tee times on the golf course for all the community residents."

"Did Mr. Peavey do that?"

"I don't know if Paul carried out my suggestion. I mention this now only because it may have a bearing on events in Mr. Finnerty's final hours."

Jane thought again about how much she liked Paul and had trouble picturing him as a suspect in Bill's murder. But then again, perhaps it would help Paul, providing a relatively harmless explanation for the argument in his office. People didn't kill over tee times, surely. All Paul needed to do was tell the truth about his meeting after dinner with Bill.

Detective Fitz rose from the couch. "I have your contact information. We'll be in touch if we have follow-up questions. My advice to you, Mrs. Darrowfield, is to go home. Your work here, such as it was, is done."

Jane saw him to the door, then went back to the kitchen and looked at the digital clock on the microwave. She had to get going if she was going to be on time, dressed, and properly made up for her first date in forty-two years. She picked up her pocketbook off the counter and headed for the door.

As Jane strode through the archway to the parking lot, Paul Peavey stepped out from the entranceway to his office.

"Jane. I was just coming to find you. It is urgent we talk."

"I'm late to an appointment." Jane took a step along the walk.

"It will take only a minute." Paul's tone was pleading.

There was no one nearby. "Walk me to my car," she said.

Paul's shoulders slumped with relief. When Jane moved again, he fell in step beside her. "You're not going home, are you?"

Jane held up her pocketbook, the only thing she carried. It was large, but not large enough to hold everything she'd brought. "I am going home, for the evening. But we should talk about ending my assignment. I think, for good or for ill, my work here is done. Or, at least, the assignment you brought me here to fulfill is no longer relevant."

"No," Paul protested. "Not at all. I brought you here because the community was unsettled. The community is more unsettled than ever."

"You hired me to help you understand and solve a problem," Jane corrected gently. "Whatever happens, with Bill dead and the residents in shock from his murder, I doubt you'll have any more water balloon fights."

"But that's it. The residents are in shock. I need someone in the community to let me know what's going on and how we can help them."

"You're not looking for someone with my skills."

"You're here now. You've made connections. A stranger arriving in the midst of all this will never discover what you will. You get us. That thing with

Mike and Bill and their power was brilliant. Please tell me you'll stay."

Jane didn't think her suggestion had been brilliant. It felt, in light of the events of the day, more and more like a stab in the dark. With Bill gone, they would never know if it would have worked. They'd reached Old Reliable, which had been sitting in the sun all day. Jane opened the door to stow her pocketbook on the passenger seat, and the hot air blasted her in the face. She turned back to face Peavey. "That's not all, is it?"

"No." He hung his head. "That state police detective thinks I killed Bill. I'm sure of it. I have to find out who did it. I want you to keep your ears and eyes open. Tell me what you hear—witness accounts, half-baked theories, anything."

"I didn't come here to spy on people." She sort of had, but with a reason, and not with the intention of reporting everything back to Paul.

"Please."

Jane considered him. Could he have been the person she saw on the golf course? He was tall and lanky, and though a little clumsy, he moved with the ease of the young. It was hard to picture him dressed all in black. She'd only ever seen him in a well-cut suit. He was a nice man, she was convinced of it, if a somewhat ineffective administrator.

"Do you live in the complex?" Jane had assumed he did but realized she wasn't sure. If he did, it would increase the possibility he'd been creeping around at one in the morning.

"I have a lovely apartment behind my office," Paul answered. "A three-second commute to work."

"The detective suspects you because you lied to him," Jane told him.

Paul jumped back. "How do you know that?"

"One of the residents heard you arguing with Finnerty in your office after dinner."

Paul's face fell. "It was nothing. I told him about the tee time schedule. Just as you and I discussed. He was mad, but then it was over and he left. That's all there was to it."

"Then why did you tell the detective, in my presence, that the last time you saw Bill was at dinner?"

"I thought it would be simpler."

"And yet it's made things very much more complicated. Did you put this in a police statement you signed?"

Paul nodded yes, miserably.

"You have to correct it immediately."

"I will. I promise. Then will you help me?"

He looked so pitiful and scared, Jane's heart went out to him. "I will, if you are honest with me. Not only about what you've told the police but also about what the police have told you." She paused while Paul shifted from one foot to the other. "Before I arrived in your office this morning, you and Detective Fitz learned something. When you summoned me, you thought Bill's murder had something to do with the issues at Walden Spring you hired me to address. Something happened between when you sent for me and when I arrived in your office. What was it?"

Paul hesitated. "Detective Fitz has asked me not to disclose—"

"The truth," Jane said. "If you want me to stay, you owe me the truth."

Paul took a deep breath. "I called William Finnerty's daughter in Cambridge this morning. Detective Fitz listened in. I dialed the number in Bill's emergency contact information." He took a big breath to steady himself. "The woman I reached, Bridget Finnerty, was very surprised to hear her father was had just died. Mostly because he's been dead for twelve years. Car crash. Whoever was killed out on the golf course is not William Finnerty."

Jane staggered back against the hot metal of the car door. "Then, who is it?"

"The police will send fingerprints from the corpse to their lab, see if the victim has ever been in their system. There are other databases they can search. For example, if he's ever been in the service they might be able to identify him. That will take a day or more, even if they get lucky. And they'll blast out photos and see if anyone comes forward, search missing person reports."

"Has Doris been told?"

"Doris is under sedation. Her family has been called. Her sons objected to him when he was Bill Finnerty. Now"—Paul shook his head—"I can't imagine."

"Her sons objected to Bill Finnerty?"

"He was married, of course. And I think they thought he was a gigolo. Doris paid for all Bill's travel when he accompanied her, their dates, and so on. She's quite comfortably off. The police plan to tell her he wasn't Finnerty before they release the information publicly, sometime in the next few days." He gulped and continued. "You see why I need your help. We've had ongoing issues here and now we've had a murder and found out we've been sheltering a fraudster. Please say you're coming back."

"I'll be back later tonight," Jane promised.

The relief on Paul's face was enormous. "Thank you."

Jane got into her car and opened the window. "One more thing. If the victim isn't Bill Finnerty, who's the woman in the Alzheimer's wing who's supposed to be his wife?"

"She could be anyone," Paul said. "Who she isn't is Mary Finnerty, who died in the same car crash as William."

Chapter Ten

Jane had been detained at Walden Spring much too long. Without some lucky intercession from the traffic gods, she would be late for her date with Harry. Since the office parks had sprouted in Boston suburbs near and far, "rush hour" had expanded to be omnipresent and omnidirectional.

As she crept onto Route 2, Jane thought about the events at Walden Spring.

Bill Finnerty was dead. Or at least the man everyone at Walden Spring had known as Bill Finnerty. What was he doing on the golf course in the middle of the night? Did he go there willingly, or was he taken? Did he arrive at the golf course dead or alive? Most important, who killed him?

Maurice had pointed out the obvious suspect, Mike Witkowski. Mike and Bill were bitter rivals, and everyone in the community had heard Mike threaten Bill. Bill's identity had no bearing on Mike as a suspect. Their animus was confined to Walden Spring and the victim's identity as Finnerty. Yet, what had Mike called to Bill before the water balloons started raining down? "I don't think you want the police involved." Did Mike know something about Bill's identity or past the others didn't?

Jane wondered how Mike reacted when Paul took away the key to the game room. She should have asked Paul. In the literal heat of the moment, she hadn't thought of it.

Paul Peavey lied to the police about seeing Bill after dinner. A lie that had been quickly uncovered. Why had he been so reluctant to confront Bill about the tee times in the first place? And why, as Regina pointed out, had Paul brought Jane in to do his dirty work?

Karl Flagler had found the body and made no bones about hating Bill. Jane had been shocked by the admission. People so rarely spoke ill of the dead. But if Karl had killed Bill, would he have admitted hating him so easily?

These were the people Jane could think of who had tangled with Bill Finnerty in her short time in the community. They, along with a couple of ghosts, were the most likely people to have killed him, but that assumed he'd been killed for something he'd done while he was Bill. Would anyone really kill someone for that kind of petty feuding? Most likely he'd been killed for something he'd done before he was Bill. People didn't change their identities for no reason.

Which brought Jane to Detective Alvarez. He was a conundrum. She'd liked Alvarez back on the first day she'd met him at Cambridge Police headquarters, even though he'd mistaken her for a ninety-six-year-old. But what was a Cambridge cop from the fraud unit doing at a murder in Concord? Maybe because the real William Finnerty's daughter lived in Cambridge. Though if Paul had called the woman immediately before Jane arrived in his office that morning, Alvarez had arrived at Walden Spring impossibly quickly.

And who had she seen walking on the golf course at one a.m.?

Most compelling and heartbreaking of all, who was the woman on the Alzheimer's floor in the long-term care facility, known as Mary Finnerty?

Jane thought herself in circles as she crept through the lights at Fresh Pond, her hands tighter and tighter on the wheel as the car clock on the dashboard ticked away the minutes, taking with them all of her first-date plans—changing her clothes, refreshing her makeup, even running a brush through her hair.

As Jane at last turned onto her street, she spotted a big black sedan less than two car lengths in front of her, headed toward a parking space across from her house. She whipped into her drive, parked Old Reliable, and sprinted for her back door.

Jane did manage to run into her first-floor powder room, brush her hair, and put on a little lipstick before she answered Harry's ring. He was dressed smartly in a plaid short-sleeved, button down shirt and crisply ironed khakis. Jane wished she'd been able to make more of an effort.

They saw the latest Wes Anderson movie at

Kendall Square, then dined outside at Henrietta's Table. The perfect Cambridge date.

They drank a full bottle of a sparkling rosé and talked about politics, movies, and books. They talked about their children, as people do. Harry's two grown sons had a son and daughter each. "I worked too much when they were young. I always had my mind on the job. But my boys were like rocks for me when Elda died." His voice thickened. "I try to make up for it now, spending as much time with them as they'll let me. Of course, now they have jobs and families of their own. Your son lives in San Francisco," Harry continued. She'd told him that during their first meeting. "That's tough, him being so far away."

"It is," Jane said, and left it at that. How do you tell someone whom you hope will respect you, or even like you, that you've failed at the thing that was the most important to you? Motherhood. It seemed way too early for that kind of revelation.

Jane didn't say much, and Harry valiantly soldiered on, keeping up more than his share of the conversation. By the time coffee was served, her mind had wandered back to Walden Spring. Harry was telling a long, involved story about his youngest grandson, and Jane missed the laugh line.

"Is something the matter?" He leaned forward in his chair, brow creased with concern.

"Sorry. I'm distracted. Have you ever considered moving to one of those lifecare communities?"

Harry looked surprised at the abrupt change of subject but answered readily enough. "No, not really.

After Elda died, half my friends told me to sell my house right away—to get out of the place where she'd been ill and into something smaller and easier to manage." Harry paused a moment. "I thought about it. Even looked at a couple of places. But the rest of my friends and my sons told me not to make any hasty decisions. To stay where I was until I knew what I wanted. In the end, it was their advice I listened to. And now it's been five years and I haven't moved. To tell you the truth, I'm not sure I'm a 'community' guy. I don't like cruises or package tours. I don't belong to the Rotary Club or a bowling league."

He'd expressed feelings so similar to her own. "I agree."

"Then why do you ask?"

"It's a long story." Jane hesitated, honestly unsure if she was going to say more. Harry hadn't talked much about his former career. He worked in security, he'd said, though he didn't describe more about what he did. He'd traveled extensively for business, often internationally, so she'd assumed he worked for a multinational company. He'd taken early retirement during Elda's illness, though Jane gathered he still did some consulting and training for his former employer.

Jane felt that if she told him about Walden Spring, it would set a whole new level of disclosure, of intimacy, between them. But she went ahead.

Harry listened attentively to the entire story. About Lizzie Graham and Minnie Brittleson. About the hairdresser switch and the peeing five-year-old. Which at least made him smile. She didn't tell him

Phyllis had asked her to vet her Getadates. That story she would save for another time.

Then she told him about the visit from Paul Peavey and her move to Walden Spring.

"Walden Spring!" Harry's magnificent eyebrows flew up his forehead. "Where they had the murder? You're telling me, what, you just moved there?"

"Didn't move," Jane corrected. "Accepted a consulting assignment that requires me to live there. Temporarily."

Harry looked as if he was about to speak, maybe to caution her not to return. Jane's back stiffened. It had been a long time since a man in her personal life had tried to tell her what to do. After a few seconds, Harry seemed to think better of whatever he'd been planning to say, shut his mouth, and gestured for her to go on.

Jane described the factions: Bill Finnerty, the czar of tee times; Doris Milner and the popular girls; the artists and dancers; Mike Witkowski in his leather jacket; and the roar of motorcycles that had escorted her to the gate only two days before.

"Does any of this sound familiar?" Jane asked.

Harry shook his head.

Jane kept her high school analogies to herself. For all she knew, Harry had been the star quarterback and Elda the head cheerleader. It was only their first real date. She and Harry hadn't told their stories all the way back to high school.

"Which one died?" Harry asked.

"Bill Finnerty." She didn't tell him Bill wasn't Bill. The police didn't want it disclosed.

"The golf guy? Figures."

"Figures, why?"

"You made him sound like a tin-pot dictator. People don't go for that."

"Since the murder," Jane told him, "the dynamics of the community have obviously changed. The man who hired me wants me to stay, and I believe I can be helpful. So, on one hand, a murder."

"And on the other?"

"I'm good at this job, and I like it. I liked helping Helen and trying to help Minnie. I like the investigating and the figuring things out, the getting involved and the making things happen. I like to make a difference. What would have happened to Lizzie Graham if I hadn't stuck my nose in?"

"You want to continue." Harry offered this as a statement, not a question.

"I do. I'm doing my first paying job since I retired. I don't want to run away."

"You want to go back to Walden Spring."

"I do."

"Then you will." The busboy came and removed their plates. "You're becoming a private investigator," Harry said when the young man was gone.

"I don't think so. I'm sure you need a license for that. Besides, I want to do more than investigate. I want to—"

"Butt in." Harry laughed.

"I want to intervene."

"You're becoming an interventionist."

"No. I think that's someone who leads one of those intervention things, like when someone is out-of-control drinking or drugging."

"So not an interventionist." Harry teased. "A busybody."

"I'm getting paid."

"A *professional* busybody."

Later, Harry walked her to the door of her house and leaned in for a kiss. Jane had a moment of panic, but he looked so appealing and vulnerable with his eyes closed and his lips pursed, she had to reciprocate.

Harry didn't press further. He turned and headed toward his car. The kiss must have been okay. There was a little spring in his step.

After he was gone, Jane threw a few extra undies in a tote bag, humming a happy tune as she worked. She climbed into Old Reliable and drove back to Walden Spring.

A lone Concord policeman sat in a patrol car at the base of the long, private road that led to the complex. When he spotted the Volvo he waved Jane to a stop, got out of his car, and approached her driver's side window.

"No one's allowed up there but the residents," he said.

"I am a resident."

"ID, please." He said it politely, not challenging or disbelieving.

"I don't have one yet. I moved in yesterday."

"Yesterday?" He grinned. "You've got terrible timing."

"Indeed. You can check with the office. My unit number is 403." Jane realized Paul was probably in bed at the end of a long and terrible day.

"Office is closed. Go on up. I'll follow you and make sure you get inside okay."

Ah, the superpower of being a woman at the far

end of middle age. The power of appearing harmless. Annoyed as she was at being challenged, Jane appreciated the attention of the officer, who got out of his vehicle and waited in the quad until he saw the lights come on in her apartment. She went out on the balcony and waved to him, and then went immediately to bed.

Chapter Eleven

Jane had her hand on her doorknob, ready to head to breakfast, when a knock on the door startled her. She pulled back her hand and stared through the peephole. The distorted visage of Detective Tony Alvarez of the Cambridge PD came into view. What was he doing here? She opened the door.

Detective Alvarez stuck out his hand. "You're Mrs. Darrowfield from Cambridge. Your friend was taken in the bank manager scam."

"Yes, I am. Call me Jane."

"I have a few questions I'd like to ask you."

"Me too. Would you like coffee? I could certainly use some." Jane led him into the unit.

"Nice place," he said.

She busied herself trying to figure out how to use the sleek coffeemaker on the kitchen counter. Alvarez sat in the chair in the living room. Finally

Jane got the infernal thing working and pushed the magic brew button.

"What are you doing in Walden Spring, if you don't mind me asking?" Alvarez asked.

Jane liked his direct approach. "Funny, I was just about to ask you the same thing."

He smiled. He was a handsome man somewhere in his early to midthirties, though his round, soft-featured face made him look younger. He had a full head of brown hair and appealing brown eyes. He wore navy slacks, a brown sport coat, and a navy tie with an abstract design. "I asked you first," he insisted.

"You know I was helping my friend Minnie Brittleson. My much, much older friend," Jane said pointedly, "who was swindled. That didn't turn out so well, but I helped some other friends who had problems, and I developed a bit of a reputation. Paul Peavey, the executive director here, heard about me and hired me to look into his little community situation."

"*Little* situation? The local cops were called here two nights ago. And it wasn't the first time. Now there's been a murder."

"Paul may have underplayed the tensions when he asked for my help, but I don't think he ever considered the possibility of murder." She couldn't read Alvarez's reaction. Was he one of the cops who was suspicious of Paul?

"Was the victim one of the problem residents?" the detective asked.

Jane was surprised Alvarez didn't know that. She wondered again about his role in the investigation. "Yes. He and another man had rival groups. Honestly, I thought it was harmless. A terrible nuisance for the residents, but harmless."

Jane put two mugs of coffee, the carton of milk, and a ceramic bowl containing various sugar and sweetener packets on a tray she had found in a lower cabinet. She carried it to the coffee table and sat in her spot on the couch. Alvarez rose and helped himself to a mug, adding two packets of sugar and stirring.

She told him everything she'd told Detective Fitz.

"Interesting," Alvarez responded. "You told Peavey to take scheduling the tee times away from the victim on the evening of his murder."

"I told this to Detective Fitz yesterday." Jane was getting impatient. "You still haven't told me what a Cambridge cop is doing here at the scene of a Concord murder."

Alvarez sipped his coffee cautiously. Steam rose off the top. "A few more questions. Then I'll tell you. I promise." He paused. "Witnesses have reported that a resident named Mike Witkowski threatened the victim."

"Everyone in the place heard it."

"Makes Witkowski an obvious suspect."

"It's no secret Mike and Bill were at war, even without the threat. Mike said he didn't think Bill would want the cops involved." Jane repeated the exchange as she remembered it.

Alvarez considered. "Not unusual. Most people don't want the cops involved in private beefs. Then again, the cops were involved. This Morris Cohen called them."

"He goes by Maurice. Technically, he called the

cops on Mike's gang, not on Bill. They were the
ones disturbing the peace. When Maurice called
the cops, he had no way of knowing the water balloon retaliation was about to happen."

"Good point," Alvarez said.

"I've told you all I know," Jane finished. "It's my
turn to ask questions. Why are you here?"

Alvarez paused for a moment. Was he going to
answer? But then he looked at her directly. "I'm
here because my department has an interest in the
victim in this case."

"You mean because he's not William Finnerty?"

The detective relaxed visibly and sat back in the
chair. "You know that? The state police haven't
said it publicly."

"I have my sources, as you have yours. I suspect
that's why you're really here. To find out what my
sources know."

He smiled. "Fair enough. Yes, that's why I'm
here. My primary interest in this case is in the victim's former identity."

"Which was . . . ?"

"He hasn't been positively identified yet, so I'd
prefer not to say. My sense is the information will
all be public very soon. But in fairness, since we're
exchanging perspectives, is there any other information I might have that you'd like to know
about?"

"Is it true he was killed with his own golf club?
That's the rumor around here."

"Seems possible. His clubs were found at the
scene, and we've determined one was missing. He
had a distinctive set of clubs, quite old. But we
haven't found the murder weapon. I haven't been

out there myself, but the scene was pretty compromised. The golf course sprinklers were on for hours overnight."

The sprinklers. That was new information. "Will that make it harder to solve the murder?"

"Potentially. The blood spatter is messed up. All the footprints that might have been out there are lost. And any fibers or DNA that came off the killer and got on the victim will have washed away. So, yes, that makes things harder, but not impossible."

"Did Finnerty fight back?"

"The autopsy is preliminary, and I haven't seen the report, but I understand he did attempt to defend himself. His killer was quite frenzied, striking him even when he was down and curled up on the ground. The state police department shrink says it indicates a passionate hatred."

After imparting that particularly gruesome and depressing bit of information, Alvarez stood and walked his empty mug over to the tray on the coffee table.

Jane thought about Paul. "Do the police have a prime suspect?"

"At this point, we have too many suspects. We're still eliminating people. Finnerty wasn't well liked."

Jane stood, too. "Including some suspects from Bill's previous life—the part you're interested in?"

"Yes. Will you go back to Cambridge soon?"

"Paul has asked me to stay on."

If Alvarez found that curious, he did a good job of disguising his reaction. He stuck out his hand. "I'll tell you what. We'll get together now and again to compare notes. How does that sound?"

Jane took his hand and shook. "That sounds like you've got yourself a deal."

Alvarez left at a little after nine. Jane went to her balcony and looked over at the quad. Small groups of people were leaving the clubhouse, headed off to after-breakfast activities. It was too late to get a meal, but maybe that didn't matter if the food delivery trucks still hadn't been allowed up the road and the cupboards were bare.

Jane used the guest unit equipment to prepare a breakfast of dry toast. Speaking of bare cupboards, if she was going to stay longer, she needed more supplies. She grabbed her pocketbook and headed to the parking lot.

She arrived just in time to catch the community jitney, the little bus that took the residents to and from town. She rode it for the two miles to Crosby's, the local grocery store, part of a small chain. Jane hoped to pick up some gossip about the murder on the jitney, but the only other people on the little bus were a couple arguing loudly about which brand of bran flakes to buy. *Good heavens, buy both. Or neither,* she thought. Was this what being part of a couple meant? On a normal day, she might have given them a pass. Maybe when you'd been married a hundred years, you couldn't be choosy about where you found topics of conversation. But there had been a murder in their midst, for Pete's sake, and there they were, on about bran flakes.

At Crosby's, Jane focused on basics, replenishing her milk and adding eggs, wine, cheese, and crackers. She stopped her cart in front of the flower counter. She needed an excuse to pay some calls. Petite Doris Milner didn't look like a cookie had ever passed her lips, even in grief, so baked goods were out. At least Jane knew Doris's favorite colors. Her wardrobe of high-end resort wear telegraphed that. The nice young woman behind the counter helped Jane construct a bouquet of late summer flowers radiating hot pinks, brilliant yellows, and vibrant greens. She also purchased an African violet in a clay pot.

Jane left the cool of the store to wait in the heat for the jitney at the designated pickup spot. The driver was just pulling into the parking lot when a man cut the little bus off, driving a slightly worse-for-wear black Mercedes convertible. The man pulled directly into the jitney's spot.

The man and his female passenger got out. She was in her early forties, with gorgeous bright red hair and wore a red summer shift. He was over-weight and overdressed for the weather, wearing a heavy, brown sportcoat. Their paths crossed be-hind the Mercedes and they kissed when they met, quite passionately. The driver of the jitney made faces while his engine idled.

Jane walked over and rapped on the door of the little bus. "Can you let me in? I'm worried my flow-ers are going to wilt in this heat."

"Pickup and drop-offs in designated areas only," the driver shouted through the glass of the door. "Safety."

Finally, the exchange of spit taking place in front of them ended. The woman got into the driver's

seat while the man ran into the store. She pulled
into a nearby parking place, and the jitney driver
pulled up.

Jane took the little bus back to her apartment
but didn't linger long. She left the bouquet in the
sink, grabbed the violet, and headed back out.

The architects of Walden Spring had tried to
make the long-term care facility look like just another building on the grounds but had only partially succeeded. It had a vaguely institutional feel
on the outside, and once Jane stepped through the
doorway, there was no mistaking the environment.
The reception area was sterile, though someone
had tried to warm it up with photos of the patients
and pictures drawn by their adoring children—
grand and great-grand. A receptionist studied
something on her computer screen.

"I'm here to see Mary Finnerty." Jane held up
the violet in its foil-wrapped pot.

"Are you a family member or a resident?"

"I'm a resident of Walden Spring."

"ID, please." The receptionist stuck out her
hand.

Drat. She would really have to remember to ask
Paul for appropriate ID. "I'm afraid I don't have
one yet. You can call the office, and they'll confirm I'm here. Unit 403."

The receptionist finally looked up from her
monitor directly at Jane, who held out the plain,
white keycard for her to inspect. It had no identifi-
cation information on it. Jane might have picked it
up on the walk for all the woman knew. But, once

again, society's views of the harmlessness of older women worked its magic.

"Third floor. It's locked. I'll call ahead and let them know you're coming." The receptionist nodded, barely perceptibly, toward an elevator bank across from the reception desk.

On the third floor Jane waited in a wide hallway outside the elevators until a woman dressed in colorful scrubs unlocked the door to the ward from the inside and waved her in. "You're here for Mary," she said cheerfully. "She's in her room. Probably quite tired."

"The police have been here?"

"Twice. First a state police detective, and then another guy."

Fitz and then Alvarez, probably. Not with the state cops, but separately. Jane was surprised the police had left Mary on her own, but from what she had seen even in her brief encounter with Mary out on the golf course with the artists, the detectives had probably concluded that Mary couldn't tell them—or anyone else—anything.

"I won't stay long. Just dropping this off." Jane indicated the plant. The attendant gestured for Jane to follow her down a long hall, passing a dayroom where a television blared at a few elderly people who sat on couches or in wheelchairs nearby. A partially done children's jigsaw puzzle was on a table, but there were no other signs of activity.

Mary sat in a chair in her room, wearing a bright print housedress. A few gray wisps had escaped from the bun at the back of her head, but to all appearances she was clean and comfortable. It was high summer, but air-conditioning kept the room cool. Mary had a blanket spread across her lap.

"You have a visitor!" the attendant chirped. "Call me if you need me," she said to Jane, and disappeared down the hallway.

Jane smiled. "Hi, Mary. I'm Jane. We met the other day."

Mary's mouth formed a grin under her distinctive upturned nose. "Ah, Jane, of course. I remember. I was in the garden club with your sister. Such a lovely woman. How is she?"

"Um, fine." She hadn't gone there to argue with Mary. Jane didn't have a sister, and the prospect of a sister who was a member of a garden club was a nice one. She put the plant on the utilitarian bureau and sat down in the room's only other chair, across the hospital bed from Mary.

"My flower," Mary said appreciatively. "Violet. You remembered."

Surely it was a good sign that of anything Jane might have brought, she had picked Mary's favorite flower. "I've come to talk to you about Bill."

"Such a good boy. He takes good care of me." Jane thought she saw a flicker of recognition, but it might have been some sort of autoresponse.

"Yes, Mary. So very good to you. Do you remember how you met Bill?"

"Of course I do, dear. We went on a cruise together to Canada, and when the ship returned, do you know, it came straight here. I had a lovely cabin. It looked a lot like this fine room. In fact, just like it. Strange to tell, but it's so."

Mary's room was tiny and shipshape, like a ship's

cabin. Jane hadn't expected this to be easy. "Where did you live?"

"Why right here, dear."

"No, I mean before you came here."

"Where did you live before *you* came here?"

"Cambridge," Jane answered.

Mary was delighted. "Cambridge. I lived there, too."

"Is that where you knew my sister in the garden club?"

"No. I only lived in Cambridge as a girl. Later, I lived in . . ." Mary's voice faded off. "Except when I traveled," she picked up again. "I traveled a great deal, you know. I've been all over the world. Paris, China, Kenya. Everywhere."

"What did you do for work?"

"Why, you know what I did! We met so many times. With your sister."

"I'm sorry. I don't remember."

"That's too bad."

Jane waited, but Mary wasn't going to say more. "Were you a teacher? Did you work in a school?" Jane tried to think about the jobs women of Mary's age did that would have provided both money and time for travel. If it was even true. Perhaps all her trips, like the Canadian cruise, had been completed from the confines of this room.

"We met at the garden club," Jane prompted.

"There. And at church, too, of course."

"Of course. What was the name of our church again?"

"You know. Saint Theresa's. With the big tower. You know it."

"Remind me again, what town is Saint Theresa's in?"

"Oh, dear. You know as well as I do." Mary suddenly powered down. Her smile turned slack, and her big eyelids drooped. "So tired," she said with a sigh.

Jane stood up. Did she know any more than when she'd come in? She wasn't sure. "Thank you, Mary. I have to go now. I'll come back again."

"Yes, you go, dear," Mary said sleepily. "Will Bill be coming soon? He takes such good care of me." Her eyes traveled around the room. "Lovely flowers," she said. "Lovely violet."

What a strange and awful disease Alzheimer's was. Mary couldn't comprehend that Bill was dead, but she remembered the name of her favorite flower.

The chipper attendant let Jane out the locked door. "Come again. She doesn't get that many visitors, and now her most faithful is gone forever."

The visit left Jane depressed. Mary was no worse than she'd expected, and seemed well cared for. It was the specter of her, unmoored, adrift in the world on her Canadian cruise. Who cared what happened to her now that Bill was dead? It wasn't Jane's problem, but that was exactly what was wrong. Whose problem was she? Jane wanted to know.

Chapter Twelve

When Jane left the long-term care facility, the pathways of Walden Spring were clogged with residents headed to lunch. Jane joined the throng. Deliveries must have started again; choices for lunch were a plentiful array of salads, sandwiches, and summer soups.

Most people were back attending the meal. Notable exceptions were Doris and her ladies-in-waiting, and Evangeline and Maurice. Evangeline wasn't over the murder, and Maurice, so devoted, was probably comforting her.

Bill's friends had returned. The golf course was still closed, and they looked lost without their leader or access to their primary activity. Conversation surged, but Jane didn't hear anything she hadn't heard before.

Back at her apartment, Jane picked up the brightly colored bouquet and headed to Doris's unit. From the crazy scene with the water balloons, Jane knew where Doris's balcony was on the second floor, so it wasn't hard to locate her place.

A small, mousy-haired woman in a black track-suit opened the door to the apartment. Jane remembered her from the dining hall. She'd stood out from the rest of the resort wear-wearing cohort.

The woman's face fell immediately when she saw Jane. "Oh, I thought you were someone else."

"Sorry. I'm Jane. I've brought these—"

"Yes. I've seen you around. I'm Candace." She took the bouquet and edged back into Doris's apartment. Jane followed, closing the door behind her. "The girls were all here this morning and stayed for lunch," Candace said. "They've gone to get cleaned up and such, and they left me here in case Doris woke up and to—" She gestured across the open plan of the living room, dining room, and kitchen of Doris's sumptuous Emerson unit. There were plates, coffee cups, and glasses on every surface; piles of used tissue near the armchair where Doris must have sat; and an overflowing ashtray out on the balcony.

"Let me help you." Jane grabbed an armload of dishes and started moving them toward the kitchen. Candace nodded her thanks as she put the flowers in a vase.

"This must be hard on Doris," Jane said as she stood at the sink, washing dishes.

Candace grabbed a dish towel and began drying. "Oh, my goodness, yes. It's shocking to lose someone so suddenly. But murder—" Candace shuddered. "Poor Bill. Poor Doris."

And poor Mary, Jane thought.

Had Detective Fitz told Doris that Bill wasn't

Bill? If he had, apparently the information hadn't spread through her group. "Did Bill live here?" Jane asked, looking around. The décor had Doris's trademark colors—lime green accent wall in the dining area, bold tropical prints on the rugs. The apartment was feminine. It was hard to feel Bill Finnerty's presence.

"No, he had his own place," Candace said from somewhere near the floor, where she was putting a serving dish away in a low cabinet. "At Walden Spring you don't actually own your apartment, you own shares that entitle both you and your spouse to an appropriate level of care for life. Bill couldn't sell his shares and move in with Doris, because if he did, his wife, Mary, would lose her place in the long-term care facility. But then you probably know about the financial arrangements, since you're considering buying."

Jane hadn't thought to ask about the details of the financial setup at Walden Spring. Could it be important? "So Bill had his own place. Were he and Doris exclusive?"

"Of course they were. They were in love." Jane had the impression of a gentle soul feigning indignation. Had she hesitated a moment before responding? Maurice had insisted Bill had other women besides Doris.

"Did Bill spend the night here regularly?"

Again, Candace hesitated. Definitely this time. "Yes."

"Was Bill here on the night he died?"

"No. That's one of the reasons Doris is such a mess. They said good night at dinner. Bill told her he had some things to do. He wanted to catch the

Red Sox on TV. They were on the West Coast, so
he'd be up late. He said he'd stay at his place. It
was completely casual. Doris said, 'See you tomorrow.' She didn't know it was good-bye."

"How awful." They lapsed into silence. Jane con-
centrated on the dishes. Finally, she said, "I heard
that Doris's sons didn't approve of Bill. That must
have been difficult."

Candace took the last plate from the dish rack.
"I don't think Doris knew why her sons were
against Bill. He was married, of course. That may
have been it. And Doris's husband left her very
well off. Her sons may have worried Bill was some
sort of a gold digger. Or it could be it was too hard
to see their mother with a new man. Doris was
married for over forty years. Both of her sons live
in California, so they're not around often. I'm
sure neither of them realized how lonely Doris was
or how happy Bill made her."

Jane rinsed out the sink and ran the disposal
while Candace wiped down the counters.

"Say, would you mind?" Candace said. "I really
need to get back to my apartment. Could you stay
with Doris? After the police questioned her, the
doctor gave her a sedative. She should sleep until
her son gets here."

Talking to Doris alone might be easier than
Jane had supposed. "Sure. You go along. I'm glad
to hear her son is coming. I'll wait here until he arrives."

But Doris slumbered on. Jane opened her bedroom door a few times just to make sure she was

breathing. The room-darkening shades were down, and Jane could just make out the tiny figure on the bed, who occasionally moved but never showed the slightest sign of awakening.

While she was on her own, Jane checked out the apartment. There were pictures everywhere—an old photo showing a young couple with two little boys, one chubby, one slender. Doris, her late husband, and their two sons, Jane assumed. There were loads more photos of the boys: as youngsters, on winning sports teams, graduating, getting married. The little chubby one looked strangely familiar. There was a portrait of Doris's late husband in judicial robes—so he had been a judge—and vacation pictures of them in exotic locales. There were no pictures of Bill, which struck Jane as odd, given the amount of time he and Doris spent together. There must have been photos taken on outings or at parties. There were phones snapping photos everywhere these days. But perhaps Bill, who wasn't really Bill, had a reason for avoiding the camera.

Jane picked up one of the glossy magazines fanned out on the glass coffee table and read.

At five of three, there was an angry banging on the door. A man's voice shouted, "Open up! Let me see my mother." Jane opened the door as quickly as she could get to it.

Out in the hall stood a red-faced man in his early forties. A familiar-looking man in a shabby sport coat. He was shadowed by a harassed-looking Paul Peavey.

"Let me in," the man demanded. "Where's my mother?" The man charged across the living room, following Jane's pointing finger to the bedroom. "Mama!"

"What's going on?" she whispered to Paul.

"He's mad about the whole mother's-boyfriend-being-murdered thing. I thought I was going to have to scrape him off my office ceiling. I'm afraid of what's going to happen when Detective Fitz tells Doris that Bill Finnerty wasn't Bill Finnerty."

"When did he get here?" Jane cocked her head toward the bedroom.

"About forty-five minutes ago." Peavey kept his voice low. "I thought I'd never get him out of my office. You'd think he'd want to get right to his mother. Why do you ask?"

"Because I could swear I saw him at Crosby's this morning. I wonder why it took him so long to get here."

They could hear the man in the bedroom shouting, "Mama! Mama!"

"Go away," Doris's sleepy voice replied.

When Doris's son stalked out of the bedroom, Jane crossed the room and held out her hand. "Jane Darrowfield. I—"

"Elliott Milner. I'm here now, so you can go along and take that useless piece of protoplasm cowering in the corner with you."

Jane grabbed Paul by the arm and hustled him out the door. Behind them, the lock tumbled and the deadbolt slammed. Once they were outside, Paul charged down the path toward the clubhouse, and Jane followed. "That was unpleasant," she said.

"Yes," Paul agreed, "and it wasn't even the most unpleasant part of my day." Jane gave him a questioning look, and he went on. "I told Detective Fitz I met with Bill after dinner the night he was murdered. I told him we argued. Fitz wasn't happy. I think he's zeroing in on me."

"What's your motive for killing Bill Finnerty?"

Paul shrugged. "He disrupted the community. Everyone was angry and expected me to fix it."

"By murdering him? That seems extreme and unlikely to settle the community. Are you sure there isn't some other reason Detective Fitz might suspect you?"

"I swear I didn't kill Bill." Paul swiveled around and stalked across the quad toward his office.

He hadn't exactly answered her question.

The clubhouse was quiet. Jane peeked into the art room, but no one was there. The artists were mostly a morning crowd, off doing their own thing in the afternoons. Next door, though, Mike's gang was in the game room. All the men except Mike were seated at the poker table, playing a near-silent game. Mike sat at a card table off to the side, counting a pile of cash. She recognized the wooden box in front of him. It was the same one she'd seen under his arm the day before when he'd locked up the game room the day of the murder.

There was a whiskey bottle and a shot glass on the table next to the money. Jane walked right up to Mike. Perhaps it was rude. Certainly the card players were surprised. But they didn't own the room. It belonged to the community. She had as much right to be there as they did.

Mike looked up from his counting. "Howdy."

He stood, got a chair, and placed it opposite him at the table. Then he went to the bar and got another shot glass. "We're having an Irish wake. A proper send-off for a Finnerty."

"I still say he was a jerk," Leon yelled from the other table with as much force as his breathing problems allowed.

"I told ya," Mike commanded, "no speaking ill of the dead."

"Mike, I'm Jane."

"I know who you are. And I know why you're here."

Just what Karl Flagler had said yesterday. Was she the worst-kept secret ever?

"You're considering buying," Mike continued. "But I'd guess the last couple of days have given you a lot to think about."

Oh, he knew *that* reason she was here. Perhaps he wasn't as tuned in as she'd supposed. "You didn't seem to like Bill very much," Jane said. "Why the wake?"

"Bill was okay. He and I were trying to keep the place lively. Doris is a pain, but Bill and I, we were having fun." Mike took the whiskey bottle and filled their glasses. He held up his own, and Jane raised hers. "To Bill Finnerty. I hope he's in a better place." Mike swallowed the contents of his glass. Jane did the same, initially worried she would choke or cough, but it was excellent whiskey and went down easily.

Mike refilled the glasses and went back to counting the money. "Took up a little collection," he said, "for flowers. I imagine Doris will have some kind of a do."

It seemed like way too much money for flowers. Jane wondered how many citizens of Walden Spring, approached by Mike's leather-clad gang, considered their contributions voluntary.

"Mike, that day with the motorcycles and the water balloons, when Doris told Bill to call the police, it sounded to me like you thought Bill wouldn't want the police here. Why did you think that?"

Mike's cell phone buzzed. He swore. "Excuse my French." He took the phone out of his pocket and squinted at the display. "I gotta go." He picked up his glass, downed the whiskey, and indicated Jane should do the same. He stuffed the bills into a cloth bag, put the bag in the wooden box, and locked it. He put the box under his arm, stopped to murmur something to the guys at the poker table, and walked out of the room.

Jane left, too. The two glasses of whiskey had hit her harder than she'd expected. "Bye." She nodded to Mike's guys on the way out.

Outside, the bushes along the path to the quad cast deep shadows. Jane heard footsteps behind her. Between the booze and the late afternoon heat, she wasn't moving quickly. She expected the person behind her to overtake. But they didn't. She turned and looked. No one was there.

Then she heard them again. The footsteps. She whirled around and saw nothing but the waving branch of an evergreen behind her. She sped up. A few more seconds and she'd be in the open quad. No bushes to hide behind. Whoever it was would have to show themselves.

Jane reached the open part of the quad and fast-walked across it, turning again at the midpoint but seeing no one. At her building, she used her key-card at the front door. Inside, she punched the elevator button. Before the elevator arrived, she looked out through the glass front door. No one in sight. "Stop being silly," she muttered to herself. The elevator door finally opened and Jane stepped in, jabbing the button for her floor.

In the apartment, she locked the door and threw the deadbolt. She stood in the center of the living room and willed her heart to stop pounding. What was happening to her? Had someone fol-lowed her, or were the footsteps the product of her imagination, overactive and overwrought, a de-ferred reaction to the murder? "Get ahold of your-self, Jane."

She got some ice water, sat in her spot on the couch, and tried to calm herself by opening her book, but the effects of the last two days, aided by the whiskey, got the better of her. She curled up and fell asleep.

Sometime in the night she awoke, slipped into her light-blue summer nightgown, settled into the big bed, and fell back to sleep.

Chapter Thirteen

Friday, August 10

Jane awoke to the *brrruppp* of her cell phone somewhere in her apartment. Where had she left it? She followed the sound to her living room. The phone was on the end table beside the couch where she'd left it the night before. Not very smart if there was a killer on the loose.

She picked up the phone in time to see the call end. She scrolled to RECENT CALLS. Three from Harry—two from the night before, and the one this morning. She rang him right back.

"You're alive!" He said it in a teasing tone of voice, an attempt at humor, but it didn't hide his relief.

"I am." It felt strange to have someone worried about whether she was dead or living. Sure, Helen, Phyllis, and Irma cared, but since Jane had retired, the circle of people who would notice her absence had diminished considerably.

"You had me worried when you didn't pick up," Harry told her. "I didn't know if you hated our date or if you'd been murdered by the Serial Killer of Walden Spring."

Jane laughed. "I had a lovely time with you, and I haven't been bludgeoned with a golf club or anything else. I fell asleep early on the couch is all."

"Good. I was about to drive up there and bang on doors until I found you."

"No need, I assure you." She paused. "Unit 403, for future reference."

"Good to know." Harry cleared his throat. "I was thinking. Maybe it would be a good idea for you to go home."

Jane's hackles rose. Suddenly having a man care if she was dead or alive didn't feel so good. "No, I don't think that would be a good idea. I'm here on a job, remember?"

"I understand. But perhaps now it's a job for professionals. It is murder." He sounded a bit at sea. Unsure about how to proceed.

Jane thought he shouldn't have proceeded at all. "You didn't express this concern the other night."

"I know, but since our date I can't stop thinking about it. All joking aside, no one's been arrested. What if I kept my mouth shut and you were in danger? I couldn't forgive myself."

"I'm fine." Jane was curt. "I can take care of myself. I've been doing exactly that for a long time."

Harry clearly understood he'd overstepped. "I'm sure you can." There was a moment of awkward silence, their first. "I better be going," Harry finally said. "Glad you're fine."

"Thanks for the call," Jane mustered. How had the conversation gone downhill so fast?

The usual crowd gathered that morning in the art room. Jane was happy to see Evangeline there, though her eyes were red-rimmed and dark-circled. "I can't bear to stay in today," she said, glancing out the window. "Let's do landscapes."

There were general murmurs of assent, though Maurice responded sourly. "Sure, let's go outside. Why stay in and enjoy the air-conditioning?"

Soon they were all lined up at the door with their canvas stools, portable easels, and supplies. Jane looped Ethel's stool and easel over her shoulders along with her own. Ethel smiled her thanks. One good thing about Walden Spring, it made Jane feel like a youngster. Evangeline took her place at the front of the line. "To the ruins!" she charged.

"To the ruins!" the group responded in unison.

The walk was long and hot. As they passed the spot where they'd ogled Karl's shirtless team on their last outing, Jane looked across the golf course. There was no sign of police activity, but no golfers, either. The course was still off limits.

Their path veered away from the course, toward the woods, and ended in a small clearing. Jane caught her first sight of the abandoned marble swimming pool.

From where they stood, it looked like a picaresque ruin, put there expressly for them to paint. The empty pool was enormous. As Evangeline had said, there wasn't much marble left. Over the years it had been pried off and carried away to decorate people's gardens. However, at the far end, presiding over the deepest part of the pool, there was a temple with four pillars and a domed roof. The roof of the temple was denuded—not a piece of marble to be seen, just dirty, pitted concrete.

In front of the temple, on a pedestal that jutted out over the pool, a statue stood. She was balanced on one foot, her other leg broken off just below the knee. Both arms were gone, as well as her head. How had she remained all this time? She must have been too heavy for the casual vandal to remove. High, tumbling green brush grew right up to the backside of the temple.

Evangeline came and stood beside Jane. "Beautiful, isn't she?"

"Who is she?"

"Diana, the huntress." Evangeline sighed. "I needed to come here today. This is my special centering place."

The landscape right around three sides of the pool had been lovingly tended, by Karl Flagler and his crew, Jane suspected. But the bottom was covered in a foot or so of dead leaves.

"Do you go down into it?" Jane pointed to a set of stone stairs descending into the pool.

"Sure, I go down there all the time. So eerie and otherworldly." Jane remembered the close-up paintings of the ruined walls in Evangeline's bedroom. "Go on down," Evangeline said with a playful grin, "unless you're afraid of snakes. Plenty of them down there."

"No, thank you," Jane responded firmly. "I hate snakes."

Evangeline chuckled.

Evangeline pointed to a dense patch of woods. "After the mansion burned, the town filled in the cellar hole. It didn't take any time for nature to reclaim it."

"But the town didn't fill in the pool?"

"After the fire, the cellar hole was filled with nails and scrap, all kinds of dangerous things. The empty pool has been here forever. Generations of town kids have found it."

"Who built the mansion?" Jane asked.

"It was built by George Wallingford," Evangeline said. "The story that goes around about the ghosts isn't entirely wrong. He was a successful industrialist, founded a watch company in the 1850s. He built the main house in 1859. But it was his son who was responsible for the showplace it eventually became. Colin Wallingford went off to Europe to study architecture and landscape design after the Civil War. When he returned, he expanded the house, added the wings on either side, and he built the gardens. His father had left him a wealthy man, so he had no need to accept architectural commissions from others. The mansion and its gardens became his all-consuming focus. I've seen pictures at the historical society of the gardens at their peak. Even in those sepia tones, you can sense their magnificence."

"What happened?"

"The usual, I guess. The succeeding generations lacked Colin's focus and George's drive. I heard there were some crazy parties here during the twenties. That's when the marble swimming pool and the golf course were built. Then came Prohibition, the Depression. The descendants were broke and scattered. They offered the mansion to the town, and the town accepted, mostly because of the golf course. It became a public course, and the parks department provided the maintenance. There was no money to keep up the house and gardens, so they slowly decayed. When I lived here in town with my second husband in the early seventies, the house was briefly occupied by a band of hippies who said they were going to farm the land, but the police soon had them out. After that, this area became a lovers' lane, and kids were constantly breaking into the house. It was just a matter of time until it went up in flames."

"So no ghosts?"

"Certainly there are ghosts," Evangeline said. "There are ghosts everywhere at Walden Spring. I feel their presence now." She seemed serious.

Jane looked out over the grounds. "What's that?" She pointed to the bushes that pushed up behind the pool. They looked like a warren for a giant rabbit.

"The bamboo maze. It's the only thing left of the garden."

"Bamboo? You're kidding."

"Some types of bamboo are quite hardy and grow even in New England. Take a look."

Jane walked to the first arch of the structure and paused. From poolside, Evangeline waved, encouraging her to go on. "Go in! Everyone who lives in Walden Spring does, sooner or later."

The bamboo formed a natural tunnel bending over Jane's head. Looking inside, she could see two branches splitting off. The maze was mildly claustrophobic, but the sun filtered through. Curiosity pulled Jane onward. She walked, then took a turn, then another. She was so turned around, she laughed at herself. The artists were no more than fifty feet away. Jane could hear their chatter through the plants that surrounded her.

Despite the efforts of Karl Flagler and his crew, there was evidence of local teen activity—potato chip bags, even the occasional beer bottle. Jane walked, she was sure, toward light and sound but kept coming to another fork, another choice, not the tunnel opening to daylight she hoped to see.

Crack. What was that? Had Evangeline come in after her?

"Who's there?" Jane called, but no one answered. She heard it again. A rustling just through the walls. "Hello!" Still nothing. Though it made no sense, her heart began to thump, and she moved faster. What was that? A human or animal? What if it was a snake? Jane hadn't been kidding when she told Evangeline she hated snakes.

Jane stopped, took a breath, and tried to calm down. If she could hear the artists, they would hear her. A scream would stop their conversations. Someone would come to investigate. Nothing could happen to her here. Just like nothing had happened when she'd heard footsteps behind her in the quad the night before.

Jane moved again, hurrying in the direction she thought would get her back to the group. The faster she went, the deeper she went into the maze. The more choices she made, the more turned around she got. She passed the same clump of Rolling Rock beer bottles three times. The ground was uneven and covered with dried leaves, but she went as fast as she could.

She reeled around a corner. *"Eeeyiou!"*

"Eeeeeek!" came the equally terrified response.

It was Candace, in her trademark tracksuit, a dark brown one today. How had she gotten in there? She hadn't arrived with the artists.

Jane inhaled deeply, trying to slow her heart rate and tame her ragged breathing. "You scared me half to death. Didn't you hear me calling?"

"I did, but I didn't want anyone to hear me calling back. I was hoping for a word in private." Candace kept her voice so low, Jane had to bend her head toward her to hear.

"I can think of several other ways to accomplish that. Did you follow me in the quad yesterday?"

"The quad? No. I'm sorry." Candace hesitated. Jane waited. Candace had gone to a lot of trouble to find her alone, and Jane knew she'd continue talking sooner or later. Candace took a deep breath. "I wanted to tell you. I saw him, too. The man you saw walking across the golf course the night of Bill's murder."

"How did you know I'd seen a man on the golf course?"

"You told the people at your table at lunch the other day, and someone told someone. They eventually told someone who told me. That's the way it works around here."

Although Jane was certain of what she'd seen, it

was nice to have the corroboration. "Did you tell the police?"

"No." Candace looked away. "I'm not what you'd call a reliable witness."

"They don't think any of us are." Jane thought about Detective Fitz's questions about her eyesight and memory.

"This is different." Candace stared down at her hands, then looked back at Jane, resolute. "I have a mental illness, a long history of delusions, paranoia. My condition is well controlled by medication now, but if I told them about the man, no one would ever believe me."

Really. This was a startling piece of information. Candace's association with the popular crowd seemed even more unlikely.

"Then why tell me?"

"Because it's not the first time that I've seen him. He walks the golf course almost every night around the same time—one a.m."

"A shadowy figure walks out onto the golf course almost every night?"

"You see how it sounds. And I know the stories about the ghosts. That's why I can't tell anyone."

"You're sure you don't know who he is?"

"I've never seen his face."

Jane had a thought. "Have you seen him since the murder?"

"No. That's the oddest part of all. Because I saw him most nights before Bill was killed."

What to make of this? If Jane hadn't seen the figure herself, she might have doubted Candace, given what she'd told of her history. Someone was walking on the golf course the night of Bill Finnerty's murder. Jane had seen him with her own eyes. Was he the murderer? A witness? Not involved at all? If he walked out there every night, it put a slightly different spin on it but still made it important to find him.

"I'll tell the police that someone else saw the man," Jane volunteered. "And about your seeing him before. They'll want to talk to you."

Candace put her hand on Jane's forearm. "And once they find out about me, they'll totally discount it. I want to help. I just don't know how."

Chapter Fourteen

The artists walked back to the quad at a little after eleven. Although they'd all managed to get some paint on their canvases, the day had rapidly heated up and they didn't stay long. Jane headed to Paul Peavey's office.

As she entered the reception area, she heard Elliott Milner. "How could you have let this go on?" Milner screamed. "What kind of a place are you running here?"

Paul's voice came back in soothing tones that seemed bound to enrage Milner further. "Mr. Milner, this is a community for active adults. It is not a boarding school and I am not in loco parentis. The residents date whom they like. I think, once you're through some of the emotion of this, you'll see it's not my job to tell your mother what to do."

"But you let this Bill Finnerty character, or whoever he was, in here in the first place. Don't you screen these people?"

Ah. Detective Fitz must have told Doris, and by extension Elliott, about Bill's identity. Or lack of identity.

"We do screen people. Moving to Walden Spring is a big financial investment, and Mr. Finnerty was checked out thoroughly. Everything appeared to be in order. We're still waiting for the police to tell us who he was and how he pulled it off."

Milner would not be mollified. "Do you know my mother's talking about having a funeral for this guy? Paying for a coffin, a plot, the works? I said to her, 'Mama, you don't even know what name to put on the headstone. Let his own people do it, whoever they are.' But she ignored me and kept making the arrangements."

Paul met Elliott's intensity with maddening reasonableness. "I'm not sure when the police will release the body, and whether they would even consider releasing it to someone who's unrelated. Detective Fitz is coming back later this afternoon. I'll see what I can find out. Meanwhile, in light of these complications, maybe we can talk your mother into a more appropriate memorial service, with just the people who knew Bill here at Walden Spring. Much less hoopla and expense. Would you like me to talk to her?"

Elliott let out a long, relieved breath. "Would you? Maybe you can get her to see sense. I want all this settled before my brother, Clark, arrives. He's the one with the temper."

As Elliott's footsteps hurried toward the doorway, Jane jumped out of the way. He didn't acknowledge her as he steamrolled by.

*   *   *

Jane knocked on the doorframe of Paul's office and went in. He cradled his head in his hands.

"Bad day?" she asked.

"What is a good day like?"

"You've had a hard time."

He lifted his head and sat up, visibly pulling himself together. "Tell me, then, are you here to add to my burden or take away from it?"

"Neither. Or at least not directly. I'm worried about what will happen to Mary Finnerty. So I have to ask, will she be able to stay?"

Paul's concerned expression mirrored Jane's. "It's too early to tell. I'm sure it will be a mess to untangle. Is she really the wife of the murder victim? Whose money was used to buy into the community? Is there money somewhere to pay the monthly fees, which are quite high? I imagine there'll be law to apply, but the corporation will also have some discretion. After all, how often does something like this happen? I hope that when the police discover Bill's real identity, everything will be much clearer."

"Did Mary have any friends when they first moved here, before her symptoms got so bad?" Jane asked.

"Not that I recall." Paul shifted uncomfortably in his chair. "Before someone buys here, that person has to pass a physical that includes a memory assessment. Mary must have passed hers, but I've always wondered. She kept to herself from the moment they arrived. Bill was always out in the community, making friends, playing golf, but Mary never was."

Another dead end. "Those keycards we use to

get into the buildings and our apartments, are they tracked? Do you know where we are every minute of the night and day?"

Paul looked distinctly uncomfortable. "I certainly don't know where the residents are and what they are doing every minute, as I tried to explain to Mr. Milner."

"Yes, but the keycards—"

"Do collect data. But it doesn't come here. It goes to some giant corporation, where they make the keycard readers. I've never asked for the data. I don't know why I would. Wait, you mean the cops—"

"May already have it," Jane finished.

Paul paled. "That would be an invasion of privacy, or something. I'm sure confidentiality is covered in our agreement with the company."

"I heard the golf course sprinklers ran for hours the night of the murder," Jane said.

Paul's brow puckered. "Yes, that's so. The sprinklers are on an automatic schedule. When our parent company bought the golf course from the town, there was a big fuss, as you can imagine. Taking green space that was open to the public, making it private, and so on. The town and the local water authority demanded we put in a new sprinkler system. Golf courses are like elephants—they suck up huge amounts of water. Even in New England where water is usually plentiful, they're highly regulated."

Jane pictured the lush fairways, vibrant greens, and water hazards.

"The sprinkler system is state-of-the-art," Paul

continued. "This time of year it goes on Monday, Wednesday, and Saturday. Of course, the computer didn't know there was a murdered man lying out on the green, so the sprinklers went on, as usual."

When Jane left Paul's office, she was surprised to find Elliott Milner still hanging around outside. Despite the heat, he was dressed as he had been the day before, in the shabby sport coat, dress shirt, and tan slacks. She thought maybe he was waiting to make sure Paul's next move would be to go speak to Doris about the scaled-back memorial service, but as soon as Milner saw her, he approached.

"You were looking after my mother when I arrived yesterday."

She nodded. "That's right."

"I apologize for my behavior. I was stressed. I knew Mama would be in distress over the death of that man."

"No apology necessary, Mr. Milner." Jane smiled, and his shoulders relaxed. The deep ridges around his mouth smoothed. "This situation has been stressful for everyone, and no one more so than your mother."

"Thanks for understanding. And thanks for staying with Mama."

As he turned to go, Jane got a close look at him from the back. Beneath his ill-trimmed hair, the collar of his dress shirt was frayed. The elbows of his too tight sports jacket were shiny. As he retreated, she noticed the backs of his loafers were scuffed and he was quite literally down at the heel. The uneven wear seemed to accentuate his duck-footed walk.

"Mr. Milner?"

"Call me Elliott, please."

"I believe you live in California. How did you travel to Walden Spring?"

"I flew in yesterday from LAX."

Yesterday? Only the red-eye would have gotten him there by the time Jane had seen him canoodling with the redhead at Crosby's. "How did you get out to Concord from Logan?"

"Uber. Why?"

"Because I could have sworn I saw you at Crosby's yesterday with your tongue down some lady's throat, and I doubt Uber encourages that sort of behavior."

Elliott stepped back. "You're mistaken."

Jane didn't think she was, but she didn't push it.

Jane's stomach rumbled. She'd gotten used to the regular feeding times at Walden Spring. Along the quad, the hungry residents were converging on the clubhouse. She started toward it.

But as she passed the golf course, Jane paused. The police tape had come down, but the golfers still hadn't been allowed to resume play. The course was as peaceful as it would ever be. This was the time for an inspection. Empty stomach and stifling August heat be damned.

Jane looked across the breadth of the first and fifth holes. She knew that past the line of trees at the edge of the course, probably visible in winter but not in the lush green of August, was a development of modest, older homes. Off to her right were the sixth, seventh, and ninth holes, which surrounded a patch of rough and brush around Karl Flagler's cottage.

She stepped out onto the course, taking the golf cart path. It would have been the way Bill Finnerty had gone, assuming he drove or was driven onto the course the night he died, as the presence of his golf cart at the murder scene suggested. She made her way toward the green on the seventh hole, the scene of Bill's murder.

By the time she was one third of the way to the crime scene, she was sweating in places she didn't know could sweat. The course was pretty, and today, of all days, peaceful. She'd never understood golf. Even though she'd been pressed by bosses and mentors to learn the game as she rose through the ranks at the phone company, she had resisted. How relaxing could it be to try to hit a tiny ball into a little hole far away? That would just get her competitive juices flowing, not to mention her embarrassment juices, if things went badly. Why did people think golf was fun?

The most convincing explanation Jane had heard was from the best boss she'd ever worked for. There are a fixed number of holes, he'd explained. Once you start, you're committed. You're going to be out there for hours. You relax and let all the outside pressures go. Maybe it worked for him, but Jane couldn't see herself getting lost for hours with a ball and some sticks the same way she did in her garden, where she hardly felt the passage of time.

As the path wound toward the green on seven,

Jane felt anything but relaxed. The situation was
the opposite of the bamboo maze. There she was
hidden, but people were nearby. Here she was out
in the wide open, visible from the quad and the
dining room, if anyone happened to look. So she
shouldn't have been nervous. But there was something frightening about exploring the spot where
someone had so recently been murdered.

When she reached the green on the seventh
hole, her anxiety disappeared. All signs of what
happened had been cleared away. The golf cart
path curled down to the green, which was shaped
like a melting saucer, something out of a surrealist
painting. The flag, stuck in the hole, hung down,
waiting for the absent breeze to return. It all looked
like an ordinary golf green on an ordinary day.

Jane could see from the path where Bill Finnerty's
golf cart must have been parked. She looked back toward Karl Flagler's cottage, which was about fifty
yards beyond the green. Karl had said the cart
blocked his view of the body. She backed up, moving toward the little house, trying to get the angle
and figure out exactly where the body had been.

The unmistakable slam of a screen door made
her jump. She turned around in time to see
Regina Campbell, now wearing chino shorts and a
polo shirt, stomping out of Karl Flagler's cottage.
Regina saw Jane, too. How could she miss her, the
lone figure on the golf course? Jane waved. The
gesture Regina returned was more of a wiping
away than a greeting.

Regina stalked off across the course, angling toward the quad. Jane watched her retreating figure.
She was attractive, no doubt about it. Jane studied

the way she moved. Could hers have been the figure Jane had seen the night Bill Finnerty died? Candace had said the figure walked across the golf course every night. Did Regina sneak to Karl's bed at night? Her body language was consistent with that of someone who'd just had a lover's quarrel. Candace had described the walker as a man, which was what Jane had also assumed. She wasn't so sure anymore.

Chapter Fifteen

By the time Jane arrived at lunch, she was starving. The meal was just about over, and she had to cajole the lunch ladies into giving her a salad and a roll. She sat down with the artists and the dancers and tucked into her food. The dining room was quiet. Candace and Doris's ladies-in-waiting had joined Bill's golfing buddies at their usual table. There was still no sign of Doris, and the women's long faces put a damper on the chatter in the rest of the room.

When the meal was over and Maurice and Evangeline stood to go, Jane pulled Maurice aside. "The morning Bill's body was discovered, you mentioned other hens in Bill's chicken coop," she said. "Do you have any idea who they were?"

Maurice motioned with his chin toward the stairs to the balcony that overlooked the dining room. Evangeline glanced back anxiously when she realized Maurice wasn't in his permanent place by her side, but when she saw he was with Jane, she continued on out the door.

Maurice and Jane climbed the stairs. When they reached the top, he hung over the balcony and pointed into the still-crowded dining room below. "There."

"Where?" Jane wasn't sure where he was pointing. It seemed to be toward one of the couples' tables, where four men and four women in tennis clothes were seated. Maurice pointed directly at a woman seated in the center of the row.

"Really?" The woman was attractive, tanned, and athletic, but in a world where so few women had partners, it seemed selfish for her to have two.

"And there." Maurice pointed again, indicating one of Doris's entourage, a beautiful, model-thin woman with a mane of glamorous white hair. Weren't she and Doris supposed to be friends?

"And there." Maurice pointed to one of the all-female tables. The women laughed and chatted, but one sat, head down, shoveling food into her mouth.

"Why do you know all this?" Jane asked Maurice as he continued to scan the room.

He shrugged his bony shoulders. "It's Walden Spring. Everybody knows everything." Maurice recognized her skepticism. "And," he continued, "I made it a point to keep up with what was going on with that rat bastard, Bill Finnerty."

When she left the clubhouse, Jane was determined to talk to the "other women" about Bill to see if he'd ever said anything to them about his background or, maybe more important at this point, Mary's. She chose the woman from Doris's retinue—the thin, glamorous one—to speak to first, guessing it would be easier to get her to open up than the married woman. Sort of a practice run. Jane wasn't surprised Bill had gone for her. She was gorgeous even if she looked a little older than he did. Jane tagged along behind Doris's group when they left the dining room. Candace wasn't with them, and Jane wondered where she'd gone. Jane waited until the group broke up and headed to their separate units.

"Hello, I'm—"

The glamorous woman whirled around, glaring. "I know who you are."

"I'd like to talk to you about—"

"You may not. Haven't you caused enough trouble? From the moment you came to Walden Spring, it's been one disaster after another. Paul brought you in to make things better, and instead you provoke a murder. Now get out of my sight, and if you ever approach me again, I swear—"

The woman flounced off. When she entered the foyer to her building, she tried to slam the door, but like all the others in the complex, it had some kind of mechanism that caused it to close very slowly. As she pushed it, trying to speed up its action, her eyes bugged out in frustration.

Jane stood blinking for a moment. *My, that went well.*

And so much for Jane's secret assignment. Karl knew. Regina knew. Now it seemed, *everyone* knew.

* * *

The married woman in the tennis whites presented more of a challenge. Jane couldn't knock on the door of her condo, even if she could figure out which one it was. If her husband was there, it would be an awkward and unproductive conversation for sure.

Jane returned to her unit, slathered on sunblock, grabbed a book, and then parked herself on a bench on the path just above the tennis courts. As she'd guessed, despite the heat, the two courts were busy, a singles game on the near one and doubles on the far.

As Jane baked in the sun, waiting for her quarry to arrive, Regina Campbell walked by, looking purposeful, with her great, strong strides. She stalked toward the long-term care facility. As Jane watched, Regina opened the front door of the building and disappeared inside.

Interesting, Jane thought. *What business would the realtor have there?* She settled back with her book.

At two-thirty, the married woman Maurice had pointed out showed up with three other married women. They took the court as soon as it was free, and soon they were deep in the game.

Jane read on. Tennis was an excellent sport to read through. The slams of the rackets, the *pawk* of the ball on the court, and the grunts of the players provided a satisfying background, allowing her to keep track of the tennis ladies' whereabouts without actually having to watch the game.

Eventually, Jane's quarry and her doubles partner won, and the players busied themselves picking up balls and putting their rackets away. As they walked down the path toward the quad, Jane followed. In the middle of the quad, Jane got lucky. The other three went off in different directions, and Bill's alleged paramour continued on alone.

"Hi! If you could just wait a moment," Jane called. The married woman turned and stared but slowed her pace, allowing Jane to catch up before starting off again. Walking next to her, Jane noticed what great shape she was in. She had a set of upper arms a much younger woman might envy.

"I want to talk to you about Bill Finnerty," Jane started. "I've heard that you and Bill had a close friendship, and you might be able to tell me—"

The woman's demeanor changed entirely. "I have no idea what you're talking about," she hissed, then stalked off across the quad.

Another tremendous success.

After the first two go-arounds, Jane was having a bit of a self-confidence crisis when she knocked on the third woman's door. She'd asked around until someone had kindly pointed her in the direction of the unit, which was on the ground floor.

"Hi. C'mon in," the woman said. "I'm Marge." She walked back into her darkened living room. She lived in the smallest apartment, the one-bedroom Thoreau. It faced the back of the building, away from the golf course.

"I'm Jane."

"I know who you are."

Didn't everyone?

Marge plopped on her couch, where she picked

up a half-eaten pint of Ben & Jerry's Chunky Monkey. The blinds were drawn, and from the number of sticky cartons scattered around the living room, it wasn't her first pint of the day.

"Marge, are you okay?" Jane sat on the other side of the dark brown corduroy couch.

Marge snuffled into a paper napkin. "You heard it, didn't you? About Bill and me. That's why you're here. How can this be happening? We worked so hard to keep it quiet when it was going on. Now it's over and he's dead and it gets out? How? Why?"

"I don't know. People keep telling me that's how Walden Spring works."

"Both of us wanted to make sure Doris never knew."

"You're sure she never did?" That might give Doris motive.

"Positive."

That begged the question. "If you cared about Doris, why did you do it?"

"When Bill first paid attention to me, I had stars in my eyes. Then I had stars in my eyes, literally. Bill often had me meet him out on the golf course late at night. He spread out a blanket. We drank wine. He called it a picnic under the stars."

"You met him on the golf course?" *This was news.*

"On the green of the seventh hole, right where he was killed." Marge shivered. Jane guessed it wasn't from the ice cream. "I'd been on my own for so long," Marge said. "My friends here tried to warn me about him. I wouldn't listen."

Jane remembered the various warnings the bridge group and her kids, individually and collectively, had given Phyllis about The Awful Craig. No one in love ever listened. "Did you know, while you were involved with Bill, about the other women?" she asked.

"Yes. No. Yes. I knew about Doris, and Mary, certainly. And I'd heard plenty of rumors about others."

Jane thought about how to phrase her next question. "I don't mean to be indelicate, but Bill wasn't a young man. All these women, late at night." Jane paused and blushed. "Where did he find the *energy?*"

Marge took the question in stride. "It's not as crazy as it seems. Bill was pretty much a serial lover. He'd find a new woman. It would last a few months, but then he'd break up with her. He always went back to Doris. He always looked after Mary. I knew that from the beginning."

"And it happened to you. He broke up with you."

"As fast as it started. He came to me a couple of months ago and said we were through. Just like that. I was crushed at first. I gained twenty pounds. And then I was angry. But I didn't want him dead. And now I feel terrible." Marge took another hit of the Ben & Jerry's.

"Have you heard," Jane ventured, "that Bill wasn't Bill? Did he ever say or do anything that you think could help the police figure out who he really was?"

"No," Marge answered, "not a thing."

Jane left her on the couch in an eighty-four percent butterfat haze. That afternoon she'd seen three stages of grief—anger, denial, and ice cream. But she hadn't learned anything that would help Paul Peavey prove he was innocent. Or help her discover who Mary was.

Chapter Sixteen

As Jane left Marge's apartment, the door opened across the way.

"It's you." Candace stood in the doorway in her brown tracksuit.

"We have to stop meeting like this," Jane joked. The lamest of lame jokes.

"Come in, come in." Candace held her door open. "Let's visit awhile."

Candace's unit was a small Thoreau, too, but hers was on the golf course side. Through the sliding glass doors, Jane spotted a private patio crowded with containers filled with plants in a riot of summer colors. The furniture inside the apartment was shabby and looked comfortable. Jane sat on the sofa covered by a quilt made with squares of floral prints.

"I'm sorry if I scared you this morning," Candace said.

Jane smiled. "No need to apologize. I'm completely over it."

"It's just that, I want to help find Bill's killer. He and I were friends."

Improbable friends, Jane thought. But there was no accounting for people's choices of companions. Any more than their choices in lovers. "How did you come to be living at Walden Spring?" Jane asked.

"I told you about my illness. I lived most of my adult life in institutions. I was fine until I was twenty-two. Then I started hearing voices, seeing things that weren't there. By then I had a husband and baby. My husband left. He couldn't handle it. I don't blame him, really. We were just kids. I can't tell you all the awful things that happened. When she was twelve, my daughter was taken from me by the state. I bounced from hospitals to halfway houses and back again."

She paused, and Jane thought Candace might burst into tears. She pressed three slender fingers into the hollow at the base of her throat, which seemed to help her gain control. She took a deep breath and continued.

"Then three miracles happened. I got better, which happens sometimes as you get older. And, after years, they found a medication that helped and didn't turn me into a zombie. Then an aunt I barely knew died and left me her house and some money. I thought I would live in that house forever, but I wasn't happy there. I'm much more comfortable here."

Jane could understand what Candace told her. If you've lived in institutions most of your life, Walden Spring with its rules and community, manicured grounds, and bulk feeding was probably a lot more comfortable than an unfamiliar house.

"I moved here, and it was much better. Mostly because my best friend, who'd been in that first hospital with me, lived here. She was from a wealthy family and left the hospital long before I did, but we'd stayed in touch. So I sold my aunt's house and I followed her.

"Things were great at first. I got back in touch with my daughter, met my grandbabies." Candace gestured toward the console to a photo of a smiling woman with abundant brown hair and two girls about five and six.

"But then my friend died. Last March. Pancreatic cancer. I was so down and lonely. I had always sat at Bill and Doris's table for meals. My friend was the one who was their friend. I just joined in."

So that explained Candace's in among the popular kids.

"After my friend died, Bill and I would talk, and he noticed, you know, that I wasn't getting over her death."

"Wait. Are you saying you had an affair with Bill Finnerty, too?"

Candace laughed. "Nothing like that. But we became friends, and because I don't sleep well, I became a close observer of his life." She inclined her head toward the door to the hallway. "I knew what was going on with 'across the way,' for example. That's one of the reasons I didn't want my friendship with Bill to go any further. I figured I'd keep him longer as a friend." She sighed. "I lost him in the end, anyway."

"You've heard Bill's real name wasn't William Finnerty," Jane said.

Candace nodded. "Everyone's heard it. I was hurt, honestly. I thought Bill and I were close. But I'm not the only person at Walden Spring who wanted to leave the past behind, and neither was he."

"Did Bill ever say or do anything that you think could help the police figure out who he was or why he was using a fake identity?"

"No," Candace answered, "not a thing."

"Did he ever tell you anything, about his background? Or Mary's?"

"We talked some. He was from Cambridge, I know that."

Cambridge. Mary had mentioned Cambridge, too. Alvarez was from Cambridge. Jane's hometown came up over and over again.

Jane gave her cell phone number to Candace and promised to let her know what the police said about the man in black.

When Jane got back to her building, drooping from frustration along with the humidity, all she wanted to do was enjoy the air-conditioning. But when the elevator opened on the fourth-floor landing, she saw Detective Alvarez standing outside her door.

"Good afternoon, Detective."

"Good afternoon, Jane."

She used her keycard to open the apartment door. Alvarez motioned for her to enter first and then followed.

"What brings you out this afternoon?" Jane asked.

"I thought it might be time for another information exchange." Alvarez smiled. "Things are moving quickly. Very quickly."

Jane poured glasses of ice water, and they sat in the living room. Alvarez reclaimed the comfortable chair and Jane her corner of the couch.

She told Alvarez about Candace. "A woman, a resident here, approached me. She told me she also saw the man walking out onto the golf course on the night of Bill Finnerty's murder. In fact, she says she sees a man almost every night, although she hasn't seen him since the murder."

Alvarez's eyes grew wide and then his brow creased with concentration. "We need to identify this guy. At a minimum he's a potential witness. Even if he didn't see or hear anything, depending on where he walked, he can help establish a time line."

"You mean you haven't been looking for him up until now? Didn't Detective Fitz believe me?"

"Of course he believed you. But we didn't know the man was out there every night. That makes him even more interesting. Detective Fitz will have to talk to this woman who saw him, too. See if she can give a more detailed description than you can. You know, since she's seen him more than once."

"She won't meet with Fitz."

"Why not? What's her name?" He pulled out his pad.

"I told her I'd keep her confidence. She wouldn't be any use as a witness in a trial, believe me. Besides, no one will tell me anything if it gets out that I tell the police things people wish to keep quiet."

He considered that. "Okay, for now. But we need to find this golf course guy."

"In other news, and you may have already discovered this, Bill Finnerty was quite the hound dog," Jane said. "I've been informed about affairs he had with three women in addition to Doris." Alvarez's face didn't move. "You don't seem surprised."

"I've read about the high incidence of venereal disease in retirement communities. People don't have to go out to work or take care of kids. They get bored and it leads to . . . hanky-panky. The demographics favor the men finding willing partners, if they're so inclined." He let the thought trail off.

Another way Walden Spring was like high school. Lots of secret sex.

"Could a woman have killed Finnerty?" Jane asked.

"Is the gossip around the complex he was killed by a jilted lover? Do you think that's what happened?"

Jane thought for a moment. "The gossip is all over the place. The early talk was about Mike Witkowski. A small but rabid group believes it was a ghost."

Alvarez laughed. "I suppose there would be a lot of ghosts in a place like this."

"A specific ghost. Or two specific ghosts." She filled him in on Susannah Wallingford and her gamekeeper.

"Sounds kinda familiar."

"It should. Bill's dalliances were an open secret. I identified three of them without much effort."

"And your assessment?"

"I spoke only to one in any depth. As you can imagine, it's not something people want to acknowledge, especially in the face of Doris Milner's obvious grief. So, could a woman have done it?" Jane repeated.

Alvarez didn't have to think about it, which told her he'd considered the same question. "The key to anyone, man or woman, big or small, killing Finnerty was the element of surprise. Whoever it was must have snuck up behind the victim, dropped him with the first blow, and then kept beating him, even after he was on the ground. We've identified the murder weapon—a sand wedge with a steel shaft. Finnerty did own such a club, but it hasn't been found. With enough of an overhead swing, a woman could have enough power for that first strike." He paused to let that sink in. "Bludgeoning isn't usually a crime associated with women. But given the frenzy of the attack, according to the state police shrink, this was a crime of passion. You know what they say about the thin line between love and hate. It's true in my experience."

They didn't talk for a few moments. Jane wondered if baby-faced Alvarez still found the images he'd conjured up as distasteful as she did.

"I want to ask you about the keycards," Jane said. "Paul told me the data about what doors we use and what time we use them is collected by the corporation that makes the readers. Do the police have that information?"

Alvarez shook his head. "It's not that simple. The corporation won't just hand over the data. We need a subpoena, and only then for a specific person's movements. Good idea, but we can't get the information until we're looking at a suspect or suspects."

That was good to hear, given Paul's qualms about privacy, but it didn't help solve the murder, or wouldn't until there was a suspect.

"There's something else you should know," Jane said, "if you don't already. Elliott Milner, Doris's son, says he was in LA the day before yesterday and he flew out here when he heard about Finnerty's murder. He says he took an Uber to the complex, but I'm sure I saw him in the parking lot at Crosby's in Concord, making out with a redheaded woman, hours before he arrived here. It's probably nothing, but the Walden Spring gossip is Elliott and his brother hated Bill Finnerty."

Alvarez took notes. "They would have checked him out sooner or later, but this will move it up in priority. Thanks." He got up to go.

"Wait," Jane said. "Who is Bill Finnerty?"

Alvarez's big eyes looked from side to side, as if he were trapped. "Can't tell you," he answered. "Nothing's official."

"But you know. The state police know."

"They're not ready to disclose it. Soon, very soon. I promise you."

"And Mary? Do you know who Mary is?"

"Not yet," Alvarez said, and backed out the door.

* * *

Dinner was quiet. Across the room, at the popular kids' table, heads were bent in serious conversation. At the biker table, there was some good-natured finger pointing and laughter, but whenever it got too loud, Mike Witkowski brought the sound level down with a penetrating stare. When he wasn't controlling his gang, he looked, sad-faced, out the window. Maurice was there, but Evangeline was absent again. He seemed like a lost puppy dog without her.

Jane left the dining hall and walked across the quad. Once again she heard ominous footsteps behind her. The hair on her arms stood up. She turned, ready to face . . .

Candace.

"I saw that other detective leaving your building right before dinner. He visited you after you came to see me." *She didn't miss much.*

She must have sensed Jane's thoughts. "My medication. It makes it hard for me to concentrate. I spend a lot of time looking out the window. Did you tell the detective what I saw?"

"I told him you saw the man walk out on the golf course the night of the murder, and you'd seen him other nights as well." Candace's face fell. "Don't worry, I didn't give him your name," Jane reassured her.

Candace stared at her feet. "Thank you," she said quietly. "What did the detective say about the man on the golf course?"

"He said it's important to find out who the man is so he can be interviewed. No one has come forward and said he was on the golf course that night. Candace, you saw him many more times than I did. Is there anything you remember about him? Anything at all?"

Candace looked up toward the evening sky and closed her eyes. Then she opened them and shook her head. "Tall. Dressed in dark clothing. Moves pretty well for the folks around here. That's all I've got."

Jane nodded. "Me too. That's what I saw as well. Nothing more. Do you think there is any possibility it was a very tall woman?"

Candace closed her eyes again. "I—"

"It's the ghosts!" Ethel boomed, sneaking up behind them. "One's a man and one's a woman. Susannah Wallingford and her gamekeeper. No use in trying to figure out anything more."

That did it for Candace. She snapped her mouth shut and hurried away.

Back in her unit, Jane fired up her trusty laptop. What clues had the frustrating conversation with Mary given her?

Mary believed she had met Jane before at church. Saint Theresa's, she said. Jane searched for all the Saint Theresa's in Massachusetts.

Google conveniently placed them all on a map. The locations around Cambridge formed a wide ring—Billerica, Attleboro, New Bedford. None of them close enough to Cambridge to make sense.

Jane knew that from Boston, people usually migrated toward the suburbs in predictable directions. Those who started life in South Boston or Dorchester usually headed to the South Shore when their family fortunes improved. People from the North End and Charlestown went north. People from the western neighborhoods of Allston and Brighton moved west along the Mass Pike.

If Bill and Mary Finnerty came originally from Cambridge, they'd only made it five towns out Route 2, from Cambridge to Concord, in a lifetime. None of the churches Google showed on the map fit. Even the nearest Saint Theresa's, in West Roxbury, was in the wrong direction.

She pondered a bit, then smacked her forehead. Of course! As had happened in so many places in the previous decades, the Archdiocese of Boston had closed churches left and right. She tried the closed parishes listed on the Archdiocese website. There it was. Saint Theresa of the Child Jesus, Watertown, Massachusetts. Just a little over a mile from her own home in Cambridge. She must have driven past it thousands of times.

A clue. She finally had a clue about Mary's identity. Satisfied, she headed to bed.

Chapter Seventeen

Saturday, August 11

Bang, bang, bang. Jane fluttered out of a deep sleep and realized immediately someone was banging on the door to her unit. Her phone told her it was seven a.m. She leapt from the bed and jumped into her clothes. She looked in the mirror. One side of her hair stuck up like the waving arm of an overeager student. "Me! Me! Call on me," it seemed to say. She beat it down with a brush.

Bang, bang, bang. "Coming!" She looked through the peephole. Alvarez, looking serious. Why was he back so soon?

Detective Alvarez entered with barely a greeting. What could have happened? Jane had seen him less than fourteen hours earlier.

"Please sit down," Alvarez said.

"What?" Jane sat.

"I wanted you to hear this from me." Alvarez remained standing, arms crossed, head bowed.

"What is it?" Honestly, she couldn't imagine. He looked so grim, her throat tightened and she couldn't swallow.

"The state police are going to release the name of the murder victim in a press conference this morning. His name is Brian Pike. He's a former Cambridge cop."

"A Cambridge cop! I *knew* he was from Cambridge. That's why you're here."

"It's true. I let the state police know from the beginning that I knew the real identity of the victim. That's why I've been here."

Jane didn't know how to feel about this news. She'd known Alvarez's loyalties would be to the police, but she couldn't help feeling deceived, as if their relationship were built on sand. He'd known but he hadn't told her. "Please sit down," she said. "You're making me nervous."

Alvarez sat. He folded his hands in front of him and put his forearms on his knees. He read her scowl correctly. "I'm sorry. The state police made the decision to withhold the identity. I had to go along. It's their show."

"Imagine," Jane said. "A cop. But how did you know?"

"*Former* cop," Alvarez repeated. "Brian Pike was a good cop once. Everybody liked him. He was respected by his fellow cops. Active in the union. Star hockey player on the precinct team. But he was a man with demons. And ultimately, he was a criminal."

Jane's mind reeled. "What kind of a criminal?"

"Twelve years ago, we had a string of robberies

in Cambridge, every one of them at the homes of people who were out of town."

"I remember. I read about it in the *Chronicle*, of course. And one of the robberies was in my neighborhood, at the Robinsons' house."

"What you didn't read in the paper, but what every cop in the city knew, was that all the families who were robbed had called the Cambridge Police Department to let them know they'd be on vacation. Just like we ask the public to do. So we knew it was probably a cop. And we were frantic to find him before someone else did. It was an awful time in the department. You didn't know who to trust, who you could talk to, who to believe in. And these were the people you needed to have your back."

Alvarez drew his hand over his forehead, then closed his eyes. His voice was filled with emotion, as if he was talking about something that had happened not years ago but days. "Command couldn't tell us what they were doing to investigate without risking tipping off the guilty party, so it felt to us like they were doing nothing." Alvarez straightened up and looked directly at Jane. "I decided to take matters into my own hands."

Alvarez had such a youthful appearance, Jane couldn't judge his age, but he must have been quite young when all this happened. Perhaps just out of the academy. Taking responsibility for this rogue cop seemed like a strange thing for him to do.

"My cousin and her family were going down the Cape for the month of August. I had her call the precinct and say they'd be away. She's a doctor. They live in a nice house on Avon Hill. I parked across the street in my own car and waited. All night for three nights. On the fourth night, I was exhausted, but I was there. Just past midnight a patrol car parked right in front of the drive, right out in plain sight. A guy got out. He was in uniform. I'm sure if anyone had challenged him, he would have said he was checking on the house. I recognized him right away, from his walk, that rooster strut."

Jane nodded. She'd noticed that distinctive gait, too. Alvarez took a deep breath and continued.

"I waited. I wanted to catch him in the act. When he came out of the house clutching a bag I knew was filled with jewelry I'd planted, I approached. When he saw me, he jumped into his cruiser. I ran for my car and chased him. He careened out of there, lights and siren blazing. I was on the chase, right behind him. We were going at a terrific speed for those side streets.

"At the bottom of the hill on Upland Road, he ran the light on Mass Ave. *Blam!* Straight into the Finnertys. Bill and Mary Finnerty."

Alvarez looked into Jane's eyes to see if she was following the story. She was.

"It was obvious the Finnertys were in a bad way, but somehow Pike was okay. He jumped out, ran toward their car as if he was going to help. I was on my radio, screaming for help, running after him. There was a big crowd around, people getting out of cars, coming out of the bars and the Porter Square T stop. Pike slipped into the crowd, and he was gone. I lost him. I tried to help the Finnertys until the ambulances arrived, but it was no-go. I lost one, and then the other." Alvarez paused. It was obvious telling the story was costing him a lot.

"They were on their way back from a thirty-fifth wedding anniversary celebration for some friends. Bridget Finnerty was their only child. She was divorced. Had two small kids, five and four. Her mother, the real Mary Finnerty, babysat for her every day so Bridget could make a living and support them. She was destroyed by her parents' deaths."

Alvarez stopped speaking for a moment to gather his emotions. "I was almost destroyed, too. I felt responsible. I hadn't hit them. I wasn't a criminal who had chosen to steal from people I was sworn to protect. But they would have been alive if not for me."

"I'm sorry that happened to you," Jane said. "How did Pike become Finnerty?"

Alvarez paused again. "I didn't know it then. I didn't know it until a few months ago, but that night Pike must have taken Bill Finnerty's wallet. It was missing at the scene, but the scene was chaos. Bridget was so shocked, she didn't ask about it until weeks later, when she got Bill and Mary's effects. Bridget did everything right . . . filed death certificates, cancelled credit cards . . . but by then it was probably too late. Pike had already used the documents he needed to start building a new identity.

"The department acknowledged one of its patrol cars was involved in a fatal accident. They paid Bridget off, though she could've got a lot more if she'd had a better lawyer. I was disciplined for carrying out an unauthorized operation and for my part in the accident. I nearly lost my job. Brian Pike was never seen again. At least, not as Brian Pike."

"And the woman, in the long-term care facility," Jane asked, "is she Brian Pike's wife?"

"He never married."

"How old was he?" I asked.

"Forty-five at the time of the accident, fifty-seven when he died."

No wonder Bill looked younger than the crowd at Walden Spring. He was.

"I think you should find out whether the woman in long-term care could be Pike's mother," Jane said. "Just a hunch. She looks older than he was, and once when I spoke with her, she called him 'my boy.' I thought she was confused."

"His mother died when he was in his teens."

That seemed like an odd thing for Alvarez to know. He must have been tracking Pike, learning about his life for years.

"Have the police told Doris Milner who Bill really was?" Jane asked.

"Detective Fitz is talking to her and her son right now. She's getting the same heads-up I'm giving you."

They sat in silence for a moment. Jane could tell there was more Alvarez wanted to say. She got up, put on a pot of coffee, and puttered in the kitchen with cups and milk and sugar to give him the time he needed.

When she handed Alvarez the steaming cup, he inhaled its scent deeply and nodded his thanks. "I'm sorry for coming so early." He smiled, but it was a shadow of his normal full-faced grin. "I wanted you to hear about this from me, because once Pike's identity is given to the media I will likely be off this case."

"But why? It's just beginning to make sense to me you're even involved in the case," Jane said. "Pike was from Cambridge. He was committing a fraud. Ergo, you."

Alvarez gave a slightly more genuine smile. "I've been tolerated around here because I've been able to point the state cops in some fruitful directions. But now that this is public, I am undeniably an interested party."

"They don't suspect you?" Jane couldn't imagine it.

"No. I have an alibi. But I'm too close."

"Because you were involved in Brian Pike's accident?"

Alvarez didn't answer. "That, and some other things." He drained his coffee and stood. "I have to go. The press conference is at nine. We'll talk again."

After Alvarez left, Jane tried to make sense of everything she'd heard. Bill Finnerty was Brian Pike and Brian Pike had been a cop. And he had a personal connection to Alvarez. That explained why Alvarez was involved. And why he'd searched for Pike. But why did Alvarez have to leave the investigation? Pike had betrayed his badge and nearly cost Alvarez his job, but it had been years ago.

Jane was disappointed that uncovering Pike's identity hadn't led immediately to the identifica-

tion of Mary. She wasn't his wife. With a murder to
investigate, how much time would the police put
into discovering who Mary was? She seemed like
the loosest of loose ends.

Resolved, Jane dressed, grabbed her handbag
and headed across the quad.

Doris answered the door when Jane knocked.

"May I come in?" Jane asked.

Doris led the way into the open-plan living area.
She wore a long chartreuse bathrobe that looked
like camouflage against her brightly colored walls.
Fitz had probably gotten her out of bed, as Alvarez
had Jane. Nevertheless, Doris was fully made up.

Elliott sat in the corner still dressed in his shabby
sport coat and tan slacks. He gave Jane a perfunc-
tory nod. The other son wasn't in the room. Jane
wondered if he had arrived.

Doris offered coffee and then went to the
kitchen to fix it. While she was out of the room,
hoping Elliott wouldn't notice, Jane covertly in-
spected the shelves of family photos again. This
time she saw something she hadn't noticed before.
While there were a dozen or so pictures of two
boys growing up, all the photos of adult milestones—college graduation, wedding, holding one
newborn, and then another—appeared to be of
the same man.

Jane couldn't tell if the figure in the photos was
Elliott. The man in the images was much younger
and slimmer and had a more expensive haircut. Of
course, the pictures could have been taken some
time ago. Could Elliott have changed that much?

Doris returned with the coffee. She waved Jane
toward the couch and took the chair opposite.

"I've been meaning to tell you how sorry I am bout Bill," Jane started.

"Really? Have you?"

Jane ignored Doris's challenging tone. The oman had been through the wringer. And her kepticism was warranted. Jane wasn't there to pay er condolences. "Bill's identity theft leaves the oman known as Mary Finnerty in limbo. I'm try-ng to help figure out who she is so she can stay in nice place, hopefully right here, where she's appy and at home." Doris didn't react positively r negatively to the speech, so Jane continued. Did Bill ever say anything to you at all that could dentify her?"

"The police have already asked me about this. I hought she was his wife, as everyone here did," Doris answered. "Now I understand he never mar-ied. He and I didn't talk much about Mary. As ou can imagine, in the circumstances, or in what I hought were the circumstances, I didn't want to pend much time discussing her."

"Did you discuss the other women Bill saw?"

The bluntness of the question didn't rattle Doris. cross the room, Elliott stared intently at his phone. No, we didn't discuss that, either."

"Did you know who these other women were?"

"As I understand it, you've already approached everal of them."

The ruthless efficiency of the Walden Spring grapevine.

Doris leaned forward in her chair, making sure he had Jane's full attention. A red flush beamed hrough the heavy makeup. "I wasn't Bill's wife. Ie was my friend, my companion. I cared for Bill, nd I know he cared for me. But it wasn't a mar-

riage. A marriage is in sickness and in health, fo
better or for worse. That's what I had with my hu
band, the judge, my boys' father. I nursed hi
through lung cancer. Some days I wished I coul
die first so I wouldn't have to watch him suffer.

"Here's the only thing I know for certain abou
Mary Finnerty. Bill loved her and was fiercely loy
to her." Doris tipped her head, acknowledgin
Jane's reaction. "I said loyal, not faithful," she cla
ified. "I know he loved her, because he told me s
and because he showed it in every interaction h
had with her, everything he did for her."

"Hey, wait up!"

Jane had taken the stairs from Doris's second
floor apartment and stood in the quad, trying t
figure out what to do next, when Elliott hailed he
Elliott started speaking before Jane had full
turned around.

"After he told my mother the identity of th
scumbag this morning, that detective called m
into the hallway for a 'private conversation.' " E
liott inhaled, pulling himself to his greatest heigh
which wasn't much more than Jane's. "You kno
what they wanted to ask me?"

Jane shook her head, though she had an inklin

"They wanted me to confirm I was in the are
before the scumbag's body was found. Before h
was even murdered. They'd already checked m
flights and tried to find the Uber driver. Who tol
them to check? You're the only person who claime
to have seen me before I got to Walden Spring."

was hot in the quad, and they were standing in the sun. Sweat beaded on Elliott's forehead.

"Any number of people could have told them to check," Jane answered, sweating a little herself. "I'm sure it was a routine part of their inquiries." She cleared her throat. "But I did see you in town Thursday morning, didn't I?"

"Not that it's any of your business, but I was in Sudbury for a few days before all this happened. On business."

Sudbury was the next town over from Concord, where Doris brought up her family with the judge and lived until moving to Walden Spring.

"I asked the cops not to tell my mother," he continued. "She'd be crushed that I was in the neighborhood and didn't call her. I'm asking you the same."

"What did Detective Fitz say?"

"He said if my alibi for Wednesday night and Thursday morning checks out and I had nothing to do with the scumbag's murder, Mama didn't need to know."

Doris didn't seem all that crushable. She wasn't the type to have a meltdown if an offspring passed within ten miles and didn't give her a ring. But Jane didn't feel the need to say anything about Elliott's whereabouts to Doris. If it was relevant to the murder, it would all come out soon enough.

"Okay," she said. "Your mother won't hear it from me."

Elliott wiped the sweat off his forehead with his hand. "Thanks," he said, heading back into the building. "Thank you."

Chapter Eighteen

After Elliott left, Jane walked resolutely to Old Reliable in the Walden Spring lot. She started the car up and drove to Watertown.

She recognized the former Saint Theresa of the Child Jesus as soon as she saw it. She'd driven past it on Mount Auburn Street thousands of times without a second look. The smallish former church was now upscale condos. Jane parked on Mount Auburn Street across from the building and got out.

From across the street, she took a few photos with her phone. Maybe they would jog Mary's memory though Jane wasn't hopeful. The wide stone steps the congregants had used to enter the sanctuary had been removed to create an entrance to a garage under the structure. It made the building look like it had been violently disfigured, as if its jaw had been amputated.

Although the church was no more, perhaps if Jane could experience the neighborhood, she might understand more about Mary. But the inter section was a total mixed bag. Stately homes stood on the street heading north from the church, two-family houses and small singles to the south. Mount Auburn Street was a hodgepodge of commercial establishments, homes, apartment buildings, and the enormous Saint James Armenian Church complex, kitty-corner to the former Saint Theresa's. Without an address, for Mary's home, even if this was her old parish, Jane wouldn't learn much.

As she stood on the corner, looking befuddled, a sweet-faced elderly woman walked toward her headed to the still open and active Saint James Armenian. "Are you lost?" she asked.

"No. Thanks for asking. I've met someone who used to attend Saint Theresa's and I'm trying to learn something about it."

The old woman looked across the street, her mouth pulled down with obvious distaste. "Such a shame." She clucked her tongue. "My best friend used to take me there on Christmas Eve for midnight Mass. Wonderful choir, lots of carols."

"Where would the people who used to go to this church go now?"

The woman thought about it for a second. "Saint Patrick's down on Main Street, I guess. My friend passed away long ago. I'm glad she didn't live to see this."

Jane drove to Watertown Square and turned onto Main Street, hitting a red light at every intersection until she reached the red brick edifice that was Saint Patrick's. While Saint Theresa's had been cozy and burrowed into its landscape, Saint

Patrick's was soaring and prepossessing, designed to intimidate its humble parishioners.

Jane parked opposite and crossed Main Street carefully. She climbed the stone steps to the sanctuary but found it locked. She walked around the property, through the parking lot, and past the former school. There wasn't a soul in sight.

She snapped a few photos of the church and made a note of the hours of Mass, which were posted outside the front door, and then got back in her car, no wiser than she had been when she started.

Back at Walden Spring, Jane grabbed her pocketbook and set out for the long-term care facility. She hadn't learned much on her reconnaissance mission, but she had seen Saint Theresa's. If she showed the photos to Mary, even in its altered state, maybe she could jog a more specific memory loose. If Mary had still been a part of the congregation when it moved to Saint Patrick's, maybe the photos Jane had taken of it would help her remember something of her life when she attended. If Jane had the right churches at all.

Inside the long-term care facility, Jane approached the same receptionist she'd spoken with two days before. "I'm Jane Darrowfield. I visited Mary the other day." The receptionist waved her on. "Thanks. I'll call upstairs."

Jane took the elevator to the third floor and rang the bell. The attendant in the colorful scrubs appeared in the hallway. Jane waved through the window in the door, and the woman opened it.

"Regina's visiting right now, but I'm sure it's okay if you go in," she whispered.

"Regina Campbell, the realtor?"

"Yes, yes." The woman leaned in confidentially, still smiling. "She's here two or three times every week, usually, though she's come every day since Mr. Finnerty . . . er, Mary's husband . . ." Finally, the sunny smile wavered. "Excuse me. I have to get back to work." She ran off down the long corridor.

Jane walked more slowly toward Mary's room but stopped just short. She could hear Regina's voice coming from inside. Her tone was low and rolling. Jane strained to hear the words.

Regina was reading to Mary. *The Great Gatsby*, if Jane wasn't mistaken. She stood at the door for a few minutes, transfixed. It seemed like such an un-Regina-like thing to do. The realtor was a hard-charging, hard-talking person. Why would she take the time? There had to be a connection between the two women.

Jane debated her next move. Burst in and corner Regina? How unsettling would that be to Mary? And what would she be confronting Regina about? Reading to an elderly Alzheimer's patient? Not exactly a federal crime.

The decision was made for her by her cell phone, which chose that moment to go off. The raucous sound echoed through the silent hallway, startling Jane and no doubt many of the residents. She ran down the corridor, through the locked door into the elevator foyer while searching frantically through her bag. She found the infernal phone just as the call ended, but she did see the name on the display. CANDACE.

Jane considered ringing the bell to be readmitted to the ward, but she decided it would be better to talk to Regina away from Mary, and away from the long-term care facility. She punched the elevator button to return to the reception area.

Back at her apartment, Jane returned Candace's call.

"I thought I recognized him, the man we saw." Candace was breathless. "It was one of the male nurses from long-term care. But I followed him to the parking lot, and it wasn't the right kind of walk."

"You followed him? Didn't he notice?"

"Around here?" She laughed. "There's always someone slower than you walking behind you."

Candace had a point. "See you at dinner."

The second Jane ended the call, her cell phone rang again. Detective Alvarez.

"Hi."

"Are you off the case?" Jane asked him.

"Officially I am no longer consulting with the state police, and Cambridge isn't giving me any work time to devote to it. But I'm still in a position to hear some things, especially when the state coordinates with Cambridge, which is why I'm calling."

"Did you find out if Mary might be a relative of Brian Pike's?"

"No female relatives of any kind."

Jane was striking out on all fronts today. "Darn. I really thought there was something in the way she spoke about him."

"Yeah, sorry it didn't pan out. I'm actually calling because something else has come up. We've discovered Brian Pike once arrested Mike Witkowski."

"You're kidding. When?"

"Long time ago. Pike was practically a rookie, and Witkowski was in his early thirties. Receiving stolen goods. Witkowski went to prison for a short time."

The wheels in Jane's head turned, trying to make a connection to the present day, but she couldn't. "What does this mean?" she finally asked.

"It means Detective Fitz will take a closer look at Witkowski, especially since he didn't disclose the connection in his initial interview. Jane, this proves what you suspected. Mike knew Brian's identity all along and that's why Mike was confident 'Bill Finnerty' wouldn't want the police digging into his business."

"But why kill Pike now? Brian couldn't reveal what he knew about Mike without also revealing his own background, and he could hardly have wanted that."

Alvarez was silent for a moment. "What if Brian was threatening Witkowski with something more immediate? What if Witkowski is still up to his old tricks and Brian found out?"

"Receiving stolen goods?" Jane thought about Mike's big box of cash. "Has he been arrested since that original bust?"

"No," Alvarez conceded. "But maybe he just got better at it."

"Or," Jane suggested, "what if Finnerty was up to his old tricks? Burglarizing the residents with Mike fencing the goods?"

"Has there been a rash of burglaries at Walden Spring? Was that part of the brief Peavey gave you? Because he never mentioned it to us."

"No," Jane admitted. That path seemed to go nowhere. She tried another. "Do you know if the police interviewed Regina Campbell?"

"They interviewed everyone at Walden Spring."

"About what we saw the night of the murder, but in Regina's case, I wonder if they're looking into whether she had a connection to Brian Pike, or to Mary."

"You think she knew who Bill Finnerty really was?" Alvarez sounded surprised.

"I don't know, but she has a relationship with Mary that goes beyond being the realtor at Walden Spring. She reads to Mary at the long-term care facility several days a week. It could be a volunteer effort, but I think it's more."

"All right. I'll drop a word." He cleared his throat. "Jane, I think it's time for you to consider going home. This isn't retirement community hijinks you're dealing with."

"You're the one who asked me to stay."

"Not quite. I asked you to exchange information with me. I'm not on the investigation any longer to look out for you. Think about going home. Please."

Jane went to dinner, somewhat reluctantly. She wasn't up for a crowd, but she hadn't made any specific progress with any part of her investigation, on any front. The dining room could be the best place to advance the case.

The dynamics of the residents seemed to have

shifted once again. Evangeline was still absent. Jane had kept busy since Alvarez had arrived at her door that morning. She hadn't been to art class or lunch, so she had no idea what was going on with the artist. She'd seemed as if she was getting back to her old self the day before. Jane asked Maurice.

"Under the weather," he mumbled.

Mike was absent, no doubt off being questioned by the state police. His guys looked strangely rudderless without him.

On the other hand, things were much livelier at the popular kids' table. Doris was back for the first time since the murder, flanked by her sons. Clark was slimmer and better dressed than scraggly Elliott. Clark looked like a version of Elliott someone had pricked with a pin to let out the extra air.

Seeing them together, Jane felt certain every single photo of an adult child in Doris's apartment was of Clark. Had Doris and Elliott been estranged for some lengthy period? It was hard to imagine, given how devoted Elliott was to his "mama." Perhaps the explanation was less dramatic but much sadder. Had there been no adult milestones in Elliott's life to record? No college graduation or wedding? No first house or first child? How did that make Elliott feel, to have such an accomplished father, and apparently brother, and to have nothing to claim as his own?

As the meal ended, Doris, Elliott, and Clark fanned out across the dining room, politely inviting the people at each table to attend Bill's memorial the next morning. Doris made the appeal at the artists and dancers table. Everyone nodded his or her acceptance.

"That freakin' guy," Maurice harrumphed while Doris was still in earshot.

Paul Peavey made his evening rounds. He was his usual professional self, chatting with the diners, looking at photos of grandchildren on their phones, keeping lists of the residents' requests. Jane gulped down her meal without tasting it, not that it had much taste to begin with. When Paul left the dining room, she followed him out.

When she caught up to him, she asked about Regina. "Why do you think she's still hanging around?"

"You mean aside from her crush on Karl?" Paul grinned.

"So you know about that."

"Jane, this is Walden Spring. *Everyone* knows about it."

Jane laughed. "But seriously, she knows she won't be selling any units here until this murder is cleared up. I would think a young woman like her would want to spend the height of the summer somewhere more fun, like the beach."

"I have no idea, honestly, what keeps her here. We're a pretty hopeless case for new sales right now."

"How did you come to hire her?"

"It's standard for a place this size to have its own agent on site. We need someone who's licensed. The person who was here when we opened left at the end of our second year. That's also pretty standard. The kind of people who enjoy the excitement of the start-up phase often get bored in the long haul. After that we had a bunch of short-timers who'd last a year or two. Regina turned up about a year and a half ago."

"Turned up?"

"The realtors all know one another around here. Regina knew we were looking. She had the qualifications. It didn't take long to do a deal with our parent corporation. They always want local representation."

"Then what happened?"

"Nothing much. It went along great for a year. We were selling lots of units. Then the trouble started. Places like Walden Spring depend on word of mouth. The problems in the community have taken a toll. Friends hesitate to recommend us to friends. Or people who might have considered us hear the current residents' complaints and stay away. Our prospects dried up. Regina asked me if she could live in a unit so she could afford to stay. We were desperate at that point to make sure the prospects that did come through the door saw business as usual. We had empty condos. It wasn't a hard decision."

"So she approached you initially to get the job and then it was her idea to live in an apartment so she could afford to stay?"

"Yes. Why?"

"I'm not sure." One thing was sure. Regina had told a different story.

They'd reached Paul's office, and Jane followed him in. He sat behind his desk and fiddled with some papers, as though he was anxious to get back to work.

Jane sat in the chair across from him. "The night of the murder, what did you and Bill fight about?"

Paul looked up from the papers on his desk. "You know perfectly well what we fought about. You told me to take scheduling the tee times away from him." There was a coolness in his voice Jane had not heard from Paul before, but he was too polite to cut off the conversation altogether.

"You seemed so reluctant when I suggested it. You were much more willing to take the key to the game room from Mike. I wouldn't have been surprised if you had put off talking to Bill. Why were you so reluctant to confront him?"

Paul put down the papers. "I think that should be self-evident. Because I thought he and I would get into a screaming argument, which we did. Because I thought he'd threaten to—" Paul stopped short, aware that he'd gone too far.

"Threaten to what?" No response. Paul made notes on the page in front of him with great intensity. "Paul," Jane asked, "why did you retain me? You knew you had problems with Mike and Bill. You must've known that sooner or later I'd recommend you deal with Bill's behavior."

Paul stared at his desk. Jane had the feeling he wanted to look anywhere in the room except at her. "I didn't think you'd get there. At least, not so fast. Mike was the instigator in every incident you saw. I was hoping you'd blame it all on Mike. Or have no suggestions for solving it at all."

"But if you wanted to make sure it was all blamed on Mike, why not deal with it yourself?"

His voice was so low, Jane could barely hear him. "I needed the residents to see I was doing something."

And then the penny dropped. Here was the reason Paul had let the rumor go around about why she was really at Walden Spring. It was brilliant, actually—much more effective than holding a big meeting and introducing her. A big meeting would have made the residents skeptical, but the rumor mill created its own bona fides. Even more humiliating, it explained why Paul had never even glanced at the résumé she'd labored over, never checked a single reference or argued about her fees. She was meant to be window dressing, pure and simple. So much for her fabulous new career.

She got up without saying good-bye, walked out of Paul's office, and trudged back through the quad. It was getting dark. There were lights on in most of the units. Some of the residents were out on their balconies, chatting with friends.

She had never felt so useless or alone.

Then, as she approached the entrance to her building, standing in front of her door, with a bouquet of flowers and a small white gift bag, was Harry. She had never been so happy to see anyone in her life.

Chapter Nineteen

Jane and Harry took their wine out onto the balcony.

"Have you been out on the course yet?" Harry gestured with his wineglass.

Why was he asking about golf? *Drat. Phyllis' combination Getadate profile.* Jane would have to come clean about that soon. And come clean to Phyllis about Harry. "The course has been closed since the murder," Jane answered. The truth, but not all of it

She asked Harry about his work. They'd never discussed it in detail. "Corporate security," he'd said. She gathered he still did some consulting.

"It's interesting you bring that up." He shifted in his seat to face her. "I'm giving a presentation a a conference in San Francisco in October. You said your son was out there. Do you visit often?"

A dangerous topic. One she would put off coming clean about as long as she could. Was he going to ask her to go with him? Surely not. It was too much too soon. "No," Jane said carefully. "I don't get out there often."

Harry seemed as if he was about to say something, but he didn't. They lapsed into silence. Jane's simple response called for elaboration. She turned a few starting phrases over in her head, found none suited, and gave up.

If Harry was expecting more, he didn't show it. He gazed out over the golf course, perfectly relaxed to all appearances. "Tell me about your day," he said.

Jane did.

"It sounds like you were quite productive," Harry said when she finished.

"Really? Because while I was living it, it felt like a frustrating day."

"You found Mary's church and discovered a likely connection between Mary and this realtor, which is more than you knew when you started. The police had a big day, too," Harry pointed out. "They released the victim's real identity."

"They've known for a while," Jane said. "It's the people here who didn't know."

"But now that it's public, maybe someone will come forward who knows who Mary is."

Jane couldn't be cheered. "I wonder if I'm cut out for this work."

"That night at Henrietta's you seemed so sure. You can't let slow progress get you down. That's typical in investigations." Harry stood up. "Excuse me a minute."

"Through the bedroom, the door on the right."

Jane assumed he was headed for the bathroom. But he appeared on the balcony moments later, holding out the white gift bag he'd left on the kitchen counter.

Clearly, she was meant to discover whatever was in it. Jane reached into the bag and pulled out a small, square, white box. *No. Don't let it be jewelry.*

Harry remained standing. "I apologize for what I said on the phone the other night, urging you to go home. It was presumptuous. You've taken care of yourself for a long time. I had no reason to believe you couldn't continue."

Jane lifted the lid. Inside was a neat stack of business cards. She pulled out the top one and read the lovely script.

Jane Darrowfield. Professional Busybody

Her heart swelled. So did her throat. She could barely gasp out the words. "Thank you."

They kissed good night, for real that time. After he left the apartment, Jane watched him go until he disappeared under the archway to the parking lot.

Jane went to bed but not to sleep. Her mind churned through what she knew and what she didn't and, most important, how to figure out the rest.

A little after midnight, she got out of bed and put on her light-blue summer robe and slippers. She crossed the living room to the balcony and walked out. The warm, humid air enveloped her. She sat on one of the chairs and waited. One by one, the few remaining lights of the condos blinked out, leaving the lamps along the paths of the quad.

Time passed. Her knees and back were stiff. When her eyes drifted shut, her head sprung back so quickly, she nearly tipped over. And then, there he was. The man who walked the golf course at night, making his way along the outer edges of the quad, staying close to the buildings, just as he had the night of the murder. The break in the case that was needed. Perhaps the solution to everything.

Jane didn't have much time to catch him. She ran out of the apartment, took the elevator to the lobby, and sprinted out the door without stopping.

As Jane came to the edge of the golf course, she saw the figure disappear into the dark, straight ahead. It was a man. She was sure it was a man. He moved in the direction of the town. She'd have to hurry, or she'd lose him. Jane charged ahead, cutting straight across the course. Her thin slippers provided little protection, and she could feel the terrain change under her feet—rough, fairway, green, sand.

Ahead the man stopped. The beam of a small flashlight hit the ground, and he moved on. Good. The light would help her follow.

When she hit the midpoint on the course, she saw why he'd turned on the flashlight. The ambient light from the condo complex didn't penetrate that far. The stars were bright, but the night was moonless. Suddenly, it was so dark she couldn't see one step in front of her. She stood still and took stock, her heart pounding. She'd lost sight of the man. She couldn't even see the pinpoint of light from his flash.

What was she, crazy? She was out on a golf course in the middle of the night in her bathrobe.

A golf course where someone had been murdered recently. Following someone who might be a murderer. In fact, unless she'd gotten mixed up in the dark, she was standing on the green where Bill Finnerty's body had been found. When she'd run out the door, she hadn't even grabbed her phone, which would have at least provided a flashlight.

She turned around. This wasn't breaking up an ill-advised engagement or vetting Internet dates. It was police business. Murder. She could make her way back, on the golf cart path, like a sane person. *If* she could find the path.

How could it be so dark? Was she such a city girl? It had been years since she'd experienced such darkness. Who else might be out here—human or animal—besides the figure in black? She shivered involuntarily.

Then she heard it—the *shush, shush, shush* of footsteps on grass. Human footsteps. Not coming from the direction where the man in black had disappeared. Someone else. She thought about hiding, but in the total darkness—why? Where? She held her breath. The person continued past.

Lights beamed on outside Karl Flagler's cottage about fifty feet from where she stood, probably on a motion sensor. Enough light for her to spot the golf cart path. She started toward it. The door to Karl's cottage opened, and a man went inside. The motion-sensitive lights would go off soon. She picked up her pace, heading toward the path.

Screams cut through the silence. Female screams, close by, punctuated by the words, "Ghost! Ghost! Ghost!"

Jane whirled around. Evangeline, terror in her eyes, shouted and pointed. The ghost or whatever it was, was behind Jane. She whirled again but saw nothing but darkness.

She stood for a few seconds, teetering from one foot to the other, staring into the night. Then she realized, the ghost was *her*. Jane, dressed in a long, light-colored bathrobe, walking on a golf course in the middle of the night, backlit by the outdoor lights from Karl Flagler's cottage.

"Evangeline, it's okay. It's me, Jane."

Jane reached her just as she crumbled to the ground, wailing, "Ghost, ghost, ghost."

The groundskeeper's cottage door banged open, and Karl and the other man ran toward them.

"My God!" the other man shouted. "Jane, Evangeline, what are you doing out here? What's wrong?" Jane looked up. Karl, of the beautiful pecs and abs, was wearing only boxer shorts. The other man was Paul Peavey, barefoot, without his tortoiseshell glasses, his shirttail out.

Her mind was processing these bits of information when the cottage lights blinked out again. Jane heard a distinct hissing sound. "Don't move!" she yelled. "Snake!"

Then the sprinklers came on and soaked them all.

Chapter Twenty

Sunday, August 12

Fifteen minutes later, Jane was in a comfortable leather chair in the caretaker's cottage, wrapped in a too-big bathrobe of Karl's while her clothes and Evangeline's whirled in the dryer.

Evangeline was in Paul and Karl's bed, their marital bed, as it turned out. She'd passed out again when Jane yelled, "Snake!" Karl had carried her into the cottage. It hadn't taken much to figure out that in addition to being cold, wet, and scared out of her wits, Evangeline was falling-down drunk. Jane removed Evangeline's wet things, put her in an old sweatsuit of Karl's, and tucked her in to sleep it off. What she had been doing on the golf course, or how she even made it there in her inebriated state, was still a mystery.

"So now you know the big secret," Paul said, as Jane sipped a warm cup of tea.

"You and Karl are married! It is surprising, I admit," Jane said, "but as secrets go, it doesn't seem so awfully big. Is it what Bill Finnerty had on you?"

Paul nodded. "I don't know how he knew. Of course, now we know he was a cop, so perhaps he had more skills or resources than the average resident. At first he just let me know he knew, then he became more demanding. I gave him the tee time schedule. I didn't intervene in his beef with Mike, though I certainly should have."

The cozy cottage had only two rooms—the large front room where they sat and the bedroom where Evangeline slumbered away. A passageway with a bathroom on one side and the laundry on the other connected the rooms. Across from Jane, on a desk, a computer hard drive, monitor, and keyboard stood out in the cottage's masculine, but decidedly low-tech, décor. It was the computer Karl used to control the golf course sprinklers, she assumed. Tonight it was set to automatic as it usually was, so they were drenched.

"You should have trusted us old people with your secret," she said to Paul. "You might have found us more understanding than you'd think."

Paul shook his head. "It was never about the residents. The corporation that owns this complex has a code of conduct for employees living on the premises. No romantic relationships, and definitely no married couples working in the same complex." Paul waved in a gesture that took in all of the comfortable cottage. "And to make matters worse, Karl is, technically, my subordinate employee. When we were first dating, we kept our relationship a secret, and it just snowballed. There never was a good time to tell. That was what Bill threatened, that he'd get us both fired."

"I would think, as a matter of kindness, you would let Regina know you're not interested," Jane said to Karl.

Karl grimaced. "I have let her know a hundred thousand ways I'm not interested."

"But you haven't told her the truth."

"Too dangerous," Paul said. "You know how Walden Spring is. That's what made Bill such a threat." He stood up. "I have to get back to my apartment while it's still dark. I'm glad you're both okay. As soon as there's enough light, Karl will bring you and Evangeline back in a golf cart."

At first light, Karl carried Evangeline, half awake and muttering, to a golf cart parked alongside the cottage. He gestured for Jane to get into the backseat and then effortlessly placed Evangeline next to her.

"Keep hold of her," he instructed Jane. "Don't let her fall out."

Evangeline nestled against Jane's shoulder. Karl started the near-silent electric motor and steered them out onto the path.

"When you said you hated Bill Finnerty, it was about you and Paul," Jane said.

"Obviously, he was harassing Paul. I think his ultimate goal was to get us both fired. That's where things were headed."

"Why would he want that?"

Karl shrugged his broad shoulders. "To prove

his power, I guess. You were the one who said he was on a power trip and Paul had to take the tee times from him."

"That's not exactly—" But Jane stopped. It was a distinction without a difference.

As they drove into the quad, the sky continued to lighten, though the day was overcast. How many pairs of eyes were watching as they pulled up to the door to Evangeline's part of the complex? Seniors could be notoriously early risers.

They took the elevator to Evangeline's third-floor unit, Karl again carrying Evangeline, who now appeared to be asleep instead of passed out. When the elevator door opened, Maurice was pacing in front of Evangeline's apartment. "My God! Where has she been? I've been worried sick. What happened?"

"Let's go inside and discuss this." Karl gestured toward the door to Evangeline's unit.

"I don't have a key," Maurice said.

"There's a master in my wallet."

Jane eased the wallet out of Karl's back pocket while he held Evangeline. She took out the only white keycard and popped it into the reader. The latch clicked open.

Karl and Jane put Evangeline on her bed while Maurice fussed in the background.

"She was on the golf course," Jane answered in response to his repeated questions. She led him back to the living room.

"You got this?" Karl asked. Jane nodded affirmatively and handed him back his keycard. He left, gently pulling the door behind him.

"Evangeline was walking on the golf course. She

saw me wearing this." Jane pointed to her light-blue bathrobe. She'd put her nightclothes back on once they'd come out of Karl's dryer. "And thought she'd seen a ghost. She fainted."

"She fainted!" The blood drained from Maurice's craggy face.

"That's not all, Maurice. She was drunk. Not tipsy. Roaring drunk. Is this an ongoing problem?" When she'd come for cocktails, Maurice and Evangeline had both had a couple of Manhattans, but nothing that would produce the kind of effect Jane had seen in Evangeline that morning.

"Nothing she can't handle," Maurice responded gruffly. "Why was she on the golf course in the first place?"

"I have no idea. But I know why I was. I followed the dark figure who walks on the golf course every night. He was out again last night. I'm going to have to tell the police about it. I imagine they will want to talk to Evangeline and find out what she saw."

"The police!" Maurice hissed. "Why are they going around questioning innocent people and leaving the most obvious suspect to terrorize the community?"

"Who would that be?"

"Mike. Mike Witkowski, of course. He and Bill hated each other. Everyone knew. Wasn't that the problem you were brought here to fix?"

Maurice put a surprisingly strong arm around Jane's shoulder and guided her to the door. "I'll see to her now," he said, "don't you worry. Go home and get some rest." He loosened his grip and gently shoved her into the hall, closing the apartment door behind her.

It was fully light, though still overcast, as Jane made her way across the quad to her unit. She was self-conscious about her nightclothes and the appearance of an oldster "walk of shame." At least it would give everyone at Walden Spring something new to talk about.

She needed to let the police know what had happened, as she'd told Maurice. But who and how? Now that Alvarez was officially off the case, it had to be Detective Fitz. If she told the story of her midnight walk on the golf course, following the man in the dark clothes she'd seen in the quad, was she also required to tell what she'd found out about Paul and Karl? She was keenly aware discovering the nature of Paul's secret didn't exonerate him. If anything, it made Karl and Paul more likely suspects, since Bill had threatened them.

Had Jane spent the night in the company of a murderer—or two? She'd felt so comfortable. Was it possible her murderer radar was as off as her gaydar? If she told the police Paul's secret and he was innocent, she wouldn't have achieved anything, except to cast suspicion on a nice man and reveal something he obviously meant to keep private. And possibly get both Paul and Karl fired.

Back at her apartment, Jane dropped gratefully into her bed. She'd figure out how to deal with this later.

Chapter Twenty-one

When she awoke later that morning, the weather was gray and windy with sudden bursts of rain, a classic nor'easter. An appropriate day for Bill Finnerty's memorial service. Jane dressed in dark colors, navy slacks and blouse. It was long past breakfast time, so she had coffee and toast in her apartment.

The community room had been transformed for the memorial service, a process Jane suspected happened all too frequently at Walden Spring. On a table in the front of the room, a photo of the deceased was flanked by two tall vases. Jane wondered where the picture had come from. The image was pixilated from having been enlarged, as if it had been taken from far away. Beside the photo was a sign that said, WILLIAM FINNERTY, which did seem fitting. The people in the room had known the dead man only in his identity as Bill. A memorial service for Brian Pike would have drawn an entirely different crowd.

There was a podium next to the table with the photo. In the rear of the room, where the reception would be held, tables were laden with finger sandwiches and pastry.

Jane quickly found a seat near the back. The room filled rapidly. Doris stood up front greeting people. She wore a beautifully cut black pantsuit with a high collar that looked amazing on her petite frame. Had it come from her closet, or had her posse taken her shopping as a distraction? Some of the other prom court ladies were dressed to the nines as well, though most of the residents of Walden Spring had treated the memorial as a "come as you are" event, and as always at Walden Spring, they came in a lot of different ways.

Did all these people know Bill, Jane wondered. Or was attendance part of the social contract in a place like Walden Spring? I'll come to your friends' memorials if you'll come to mine. Or were the mourners just after what looked to be a load of delicious baked goods? All of the above, Jane guessed.

Standing on either side of Doris, looking solemn and shaking hands, were her sons, sleek Clark and beefy Elliott. Next to Elliott was the redhead he'd made out with behind the Mercedes at Crosby's. A stiff smile was plastered on her freckled face. Elliott must have finally broken down and told his mother about his local girlfriend.

Candace sat among the popular kids, and as usual she didn't look as if she fit in. She was dressed in her trademark tracksuit, black today, appropriate for the occasion.

Mike Witkowski was back. Whatever the state police had, they hadn't been able to hold him. His crew occupied a whole row, dressed in their pseudo cycle gang gear. Mike caught Jane's eye and bobbed his head in quick acknowledgment.

The attendant in the colorful scrubs had brought Mary over from the long-term care unit. Evangeline, looking ragged and wincing at the slightest noise, sat with Maurice. Foghorn-voiced Ethel sat with the rest of the artists. Regina Campbell stood off to one side.

Jane was surprised to spot Detective Alvarez standing in the back. She tried to catch his eye, but he avoided her gaze. They'd talked twice the day before, and on neither occasion had he mentioned he'd be at this memorial. Jane supposed no one could keep him from attending in an unofficial capacity.

Karl sat in a row with the rest of the groundskeepers. Paul stood at the back. How strange for Paul and Karl not to be able to sit together, or even acknowledge their true relationship. But the room was filled with hidden connections. Regina and Mary. The women who had affairs with Brian Pike as he cheated on both Doris and Mary. Alvarez and Mike's connection with the real Brian Pike before he'd become Bill Finnerty.

Doris's sons walked their mother to the podium, then took their seats in the front row. Elliott took the redhead's hand and held it.

Doris gripped the sides of the podium and began. "We are here to pay tribute to my great, good friend, Bill Finnerty," she said. "Bill was a friend to me like no other. After I lost my husband, Bill became my best friend. We could talk for hours about anything and nothing. He nurtured me after my greatest sadness"—she looked pointedly at her sons—"the loss of my husband of forty-six years.

"Since Bill's sudden and untimely death, you may have heard some unkind things about him. You may have even said some of them yourself. But no one is either entirely good or entirely bad. The Bill Finnerty you and I knew was a loyal friend who laughed easily and played hard. He brought me out of my widow's fog, and made sure that his . . . Mary was cared for in her time of need. That is the man I ask you to remember."

Jane's eyes swept the room. She caught Alvarez doing the same. Sure enough, Bill's lovers began to break down. The beautiful woman from Doris's entourage was crying hard. The ice-cream-loving woman put her head in her hands and bawled her eyes out. Even the tennis-playing married woman dabbed at her eyes with a tissue.

Finally, sobbing loudly, was . . . Evangeline. Evangeline? What did her obvious grief say about her feelings for Bill Finnerty? On one hand, she always showed her emotions operatically. On the other, she'd been off-kilter since the murder, and there was the crazy midnight walk on the golf course.

Evangeline's caterwauling became louder and louder, drawing increasing attention. Next to her, Maurice sat hunched over and scowling.

After the memorial, the residents adjourned to the back of the room, where cookies, finger sandwiches, tea, and coffee were served. The silver tea service and tiered china dishes were elaborate; they obviously hadn't come from the Walden Spring corporate catering service. Doris and her cronies must have used their own treasures, dragged out from wherever these things were crammed into their condos. Why did we keep these things, Jane wondered. So appropriate to our Victorian grandmothers' grandmothers, so out of place in a room that looked like a teachers' lounge in an upscale high school.

As soon as he spotted Jane across the crowded room, Elliott grabbed the redhead by the elbow and beelined over.

"Mrs. Darrowfield," he said, "I'd like to present my fiancée, Bev—" Bev's last name was lost in the din of the room.

"Fiancée! Congratulations. I never would have guessed." *Especially because you denied her existence until today.*

Elliott leaned in confidentially. "She's why I was here. Bev was my high school girlfriend. Then we both went off to college and, you know, lost track. Last spring, I came back for my twenty-fifth high school reunion, first time I've gone to one in all these years. I found out Bev was divorced, and I was in a better position to be in a relationship than I'd been in a long time. For the last couple of months, I've kind of been living at Bev's place. Isn't she great?"

"She is." Jane smiled at Bev, who had held her own in the undoubtedly awkward circumstances of meeting her fiancé's mother and all her friends at the memorial service for the mother's faux boyfriend. Or, real boyfriend, faux person. Points for Bev Something that she could be gracious in the circumstances.

"I didn't want to tell Mama and Clark," Elliott continued, "because I was sure they'd have something negative to say, and I wanted to be sure it was going to last. Now I'm looking for a job out here." Elliott shouted into Jane's ear to be heard over the crowd. "Thank you. For forcing me to talk to the cops about where I was on the night of the murder, which forced me to talk to Mama and Clark, which brought all this out in the open." He leaned in and gave Jane a hug. She tottered backward, more than a little shocked.

When Elliott stepped away, Bev Something also came in for a hug and an even more heartfelt "Thank you."

Jane had something completely different in mind when she told Alvarez to check into Elliott's travel. But she couldn't help but be happy for Elliott with how it all turned out.

She spotted Regina Campbell over by the food table flirting like mad with Karl, who kept glancing at the exit. In her black heels Regina towered over most of the crowd. Jane excused herself and approached them.

"Karl, can I borrow Regina a minute?"

"Sure." Karl, looking relieved, backed away.

"I know you've been visiting Mary Finnerty over in the long-term care building," Jane said when Karl was out of earshot. "That's so nice of you. Has she ever mentioned—"

"No!" Regina snapped. She twirled around and stalked off in the opposite direction. *Another stellar success.*

When Alvarez headed for the exit, Jane ran up to Mary Finnerty and the startled attendant, took two quick photos of Mary with her phone, and ran out into the rain after him.

"Not here!" Alvarez hissed when Jane caught up to him in the parking lot. "Starbucks, Lexington Center." He jumped into his car and peeled out of the lot. Despite the rain, Jane walked to Old Reliable at a pace intended to telegraph "casual" to any observers and drove off, too.

Chapter Twenty-two

Alvarez was already seated at a table for two when Jane arrived. It was midday, and the place was nearly empty. The tourists braving the damp, chilly day on Lexington Green evidently didn't have Starbucks on their itineraries. Jane ordered her coffee hot and bought a scone to go with it.

"I was surprised to see you today," she said, sitting across from Alvarez.

"I shouldn't have gone. I told myself I was going for personal reasons, to pay tribute to my fallen comrade. But as soon as I got there, I realized it wasn't the reason. I have no interest in honoring Bill Finnerty—or Brian Pike."

The tension in Alvarez's voice was palpable. He had every reason to feel betrayed. His brother in blue had become a criminal, killed two people, and almost wrecked Alvarez's career. Still, it was a long time ago. A long time to hold on to such hate.

"Did you notice Evangeline?" Jane asked, feel-

ing disloyal to the first person to welcome her to
Walden Spring. But who, the night before, it had
to be admitted, had also been out at the very hole
where Bill Finnerty was killed, drunk as a skunk.

"You mean the disproportionate sobbing and
carrying on? Jane, the cosmonauts on the space
station noticed Mrs. Murray."

"I had a strange encounter with her. I found her
walking on the golf course after one o'clock this
morning."

Alvarez's tension slipped away as he turned his
attention to Jane. "What do you mean, 'found her'?
What were you doing on the golf course at one
o'clock?"

Ah, there was the rub. "I followed the man in
black."

"What? I told you to be careful. These aren't jolly
senior citizens' pranks anymore. We're talking
about murder suspects. Where on the golf course?"

"The seventh hole."

Alvarez glowered.

The color rose in Jane's face. "I know, I know. I
realized I was being stupid and had turned around
to go back to my apartment when Evangeline and
I almost bumped into each other."

"Then what happened?"

Jane said it very fast. "Paul Peavey and Karl Flagler heard Evangeline scream. They came out of
Karl's cottage and found us."

"Peavey was at Flagler's cottage at one in the
morning? Are they—?"

"Indeed. They are more than that. They are
married."

"What a weird thing to conceal."

"Something about the corporation that owns Walden Spring having rules against married couples working in the same location."

Alvarez, still frowning, toyed with an empty sugar packet, folding it over and over. "Then what happened?"

"The golf course sprinklers came on and doused us all."

Alvarez burst out laughing and kept laughing. His laugh was the infectious kind, and soon Jane was laughing, too. "So let me get this straight," Alvarez gasped. "You, the man in black, Evangeline Murray, Paul Peavey, and Karl Flagler were all on the Walden Spring golf course at one in the morning. The Concord police should post a traffic detail out there." He laughed some more.

"I needed that." Alvarez pulled himself together, wiping his eyes. "Did you find out why Mrs. Murray was there?"

"She was drunk and passed out immediately afterward. Karl drove us home in his golf cart. The first time I saw her conscious since it happened was at the memorial."

"You never caught up to the man in black, I take it."

"No. That mission was a failure."

"It's probably for the best."

"I understand you can't be part of the investigation because you were involved in Brian Pike's accident with the Finnertys," Jane said. "But that was twelve years ago, and you still seem intensely angry."

Alvarez hesitated before speaking, then appeared to make a decision. Like Jane, he needed someone to trust. And someone to trust him. "Do you remember I told you how sorry I felt for Bridget Finnerty?" he began.

Jane nodded.

"When her parents were killed, she lost her only source of emotional support. Her only family. And the lawyer she hired didn't get her much from the department." Alvarez looked at Jane, searching her eyes to see if she understood. She nodded for him to go on. "After the lawsuit was settled, I started going by her house. Just to help out. I felt terrible for my part in the accident. But Bridget is a strong person. So strong. Over time, my feelings moved from pity and guilt"—Alvarez blushed deeply—"to love. I moved into her house a year after the accident, and I've been there ever since."

Jane consciously closed her mouth, which had dropped open. Then she spoke. "So your stake in the deaths of the Finnertys is even more personal, if that's possible. I get that, but—"

"I tried to find Brian Pike for years. It was as if he disappeared off the face of the earth the night of the accident. He never went back to his apartment or used any of his credit cards or touched his bank account again. Sometimes patrol guys would say they'd seen him on this corner or that. But whenever I'd check it out, no one could recall him.

"Then, this spring, I was home alone one afternoon on a day I was working a late shift. A collection company called and asked if I was William Finnerty. Bridget never changed her landline number or listing after her parents died. I was curious, so I said I was. They said they were just confirming I was the same William Finnerty who had an MRI at Emerson Hospital a couple of years ago and didn't pay the bill. I was about to say no, but then I had an insight. What if it was Brian? He'd disappeared the night of the crash, and Bill Finnerty's wallet had disappeared as well. Brian had plenty of time to establish an account at another bank, get some new cards, and so on, before Bridget got around to canceling everything. So I said that I was not, in fact, the William Finnerty who'd had the MRI. The collection company thanked me, and that was that.

"After that phone call, in my spare time, I started checking up on William Finnertys. It's a common name, especially in Massachusetts, so it took a while, but I figured he lived somewhere near Emerson Hospital, which was the best clue I'd had in ages. A few months ago, I found a six-year-old purchase and sale agreement for William and Mary Finnerty at Walden Spring."

"You knew he was there before the murder."

"When I saw that Walden Spring had a golf course, I knew if Brian was there, he'd be out on the course. Whenever I had a couple of free hours, I drove to Concord and walked into the woods by the links. After only a few days, I saw him. Brian Pike, with that cocky strut of his, and everyone in his foursome calling him Bill."

"What did you do?"

Alvarez stared at the tabletop. "Nothing. I didn't even tell Bridget about it."

Jane didn't try to hide her surprise. "But he killed two people, and he was actively committing identity theft, fraud—"

"I know, I know. I guess I thought he was safe,

tucked away at Walden Spring. He'd already been here for several years. I had plenty of time to figure out how to bring him to justice. I knew his arrest would take Bridget down that whole horrible road again."

"And when you heard there was a murder at Walden Spring—"

"I knew."

"I thought you got there too quickly."

"I didn't wait to be asked." Alvarez smiled, and the tension drained away. It hadn't been easy for him to tell her all this.

Suddenly Jane had a horrible thought. "You let Paul Peavey call Bridget and say her father was dead."

Alvarez hung his head. "I was stuck in the reception area outside his office. By the time I talked my way into Peavey's office, the call had been made." He shrugged. "If I'd stopped them, I would have had to tell them why."

"And that would raise the obvious question. If you knew Brian Pike was there, actively committing fraud, with double manslaughter charges hanging over his head, why hadn't you told anyone? It was bound to come out."

Alvarez looked across the table and straight into Jane's eyes. "When I got home yesterday, I told Bridget everything. About how I found out about the Finnerty identity, stalking Pike on the golf course, the murder. Everything."

"And?"

"And let's just say I'm sleeping on the couch. It took me a long time to gain her trust in the first place. A cop killed her parents because I was chasing him. She sued the department. Now I'm back to square one. Or maybe square two. At least this time, her kids are rooting for me."

Bridget Finnerty's children, preschoolers at the time of the accident, would be teenagers today.

"What happens now?" Jane asked.

"Nothing. I'm off the case. I'm going to let justice run its course."

"Are you going to tell Detective Fitz what I told you about Evangeline and Paul and Karl?"

Alvarez shook his head. "No. You're going to. I know you a little bit now, and you're too much of a straight arrow not to. After you do that, is there any chance of you packing up and going home?" He looked at her and shook his head. "I didn't think so."

After Alvarez and Jane said their good-byes, she climbed into Old Reliable and started her up. The clock on the dashboard flashed 12:40. If she hurried, she could make it to the one o'clock Mass at Saint Patrick's in Watertown, the last Mass of the weekend.

As she drove on toward the church, Jane thought about the slender thread that had brought her there. If she had found the right Saint Theresa's. If the parishioners had moved on to Saint Patrick's. If any of them now attended the late Sunday Mass. And, of course, the slenderest thread of all: The whole journey relied on the reminisces of a woman with Alzheimer's disease.

By the time she got to the church and parked, Jane was a little late for the Mass. The clouds had moved away, and the sun peeked out as she ran up the front steps. Inside, she tried to sneak into the last pew, but an elderly man waved her forward. She ignored him, but that caused his gestures to become more insistent. Unwilling to make more of a scene, Jane acquiesced and sat where he wanted her to. At least it was off to the side so she could observe most of the parishioners.

Saint Patrick's was a large, traditional Catholic church of the type built at the turn of the last century. The green and brown stained glass windows bathed the congregation in a sickly light. At the height of summer, the Mass was sparsely attended, and at least 80 percent of the parishioners were, as Jane had hoped, elderly. If Walden Spring made her feel like a kid, Mass at Saint Patrick's in August made her feel like an infant. The priest sped through the service as if he had a plane to catch.

At the end of the Mass, everyone filed out. As they got to the front of the church, Jane realized she had to make a choice. Half the attendees headed for the front door, and the other half left by the side, presumably toward a parking lot. She chose the front.

While the parishioners, who all seemed to know one another, chatted on the front steps, Jane seized her chance. She knew it was a long, long shot. The photos on her phone were of an elderly woman. As an Alzheimer's patient, Mary Finnerty had no control over her wardrobe and hairdo. Whatever vestiges of "style" she demonstrated were undoubtedly not her own. Jane's best hope was Mary's most distinctive feature, the upturned nose.

Jane approached a likely looking trio—a man in

a checkered sports shirt and cap and two women, one wearing a tight, white bun and the other thick glasses. "Excuse me. Do you know this woman?"

They paused, out of politeness, Jane thought, not curiosity. She handed over her phone. The woman with the bun got her glasses out. "Does she go to Mass here, dear?"

"I think she used to. Actually, I think she was originally from Saint Theresa's."

The three of them clustered around the phone. "Saint Theresa's, you say? Wait a moment. Mary!" the one with the bun called out.

Jane's heart fluttered. Had she recognized Mary? But then five or six heads turned in their direction. Jane had observed this phenomenon before. If one called out "Mary!" or "Joseph!" in certain neighborhoods around Boston—in doctors' offices, diners, grocery stores—half the people would turn their heads.

"Mary McCool!" the white bun lady clarified.

Mary McCool was already off the steps of the church and halfway down the walk. She turned around with some effort. She was supported by a woman who had to be her daughter. They looked so much alike, the mother was like an artificially aged image of the daughter.

"Mary went to Saint Theresa's," white bun said. "She knows everyone from the old days."

Jane introduced herself to Mrs. McCool and her daughter, Linda. Mrs. McCool took the phone in her trembling hands and studied the photo. Linda got out her own reading glasses.

"Sorry—" Mrs. McCool started to hand back the phone. Jane's shoulders sagged. She had so hoped this would be the key to identifying the Mary at Walden Spring. She hadn't realized until that very moment how much she'd been counting on this to work.

"Wait a minute." Jane took the phone in her left hand, then placed her left thumb over Mary's forehead and her right pointer finger over Mary's chin so that only the distinctive nose remained.

"Let me see the whole photo again." Linda McCool studied the phone. "Sister Mary Martha!" she cried. "Has to be. She was my teacher at the school here. Eighth-grade math."

By this point, Mrs. McCool was nodding. "Oh, my gracious, you're right. I believe that is the Sister."

"This woman is a nun?" That was the last thing Jane had expected.

"Was a nun," Mrs. McCool corrected. "When she taught here in the sixties. She left the order in the seventies, when so many did. But she stayed in town and attended Saint Theresa's."

"Why did she leave?"

"I didn't know her that well. Just disillusioned, I guess. Such a shame." Mrs. McCool's voice quivered with age, but she spoke with conviction.

"She didn't leave teaching, though," Linda said. "I heard she taught in a public school in Cambridge."

"Did she have family?"

Mother and daughter looked at each other, mirroring identical squints. "A sister," Linda finally said. "From somewhere around here. I heard they had a falling out when Sister left the order. Her family was scandalized. Shunned her."

Mrs. McCool read the look on Jane's face. "I know it sounds terrible, but to have a child or a sibling become a nun or a priest was such a source of pride in those days. And to have them leave was a disgrace."

"Do you know her real name?"

"Virginia, no, Violet, I think," Linda answered. "I don't remember the last name, if I ever knew it. Has something happened to her? Why are you looking for her?"

Violet! No wonder Mary had remembered the name of the flower. Jane wasn't looking for her. She knew right where she was. "Unfortunately, she has Alzheimer's disease. I'm looking for her family."

"Her sister was married, so she'd have a different last name," Linda said. "The teaching nuns here were Dominicans. Maybe the order would have the information you're looking for."

Jane thanked them, took down their contact info, and practically skipped the short distance to her car. Sister Mary Martha. It made so much sense. If Mary were displaying the early signs of Alzheimer's when they'd moved to Walden Spring, she surely would have had trouble remembering a fake identity. Brian Pike had supplied her with the one name she was sure to respond to. Her old nun name.

Chapter Twenty-three

Dinner that night was as close to normal as any had been since the murder, as if the memorial service truly had helped some people move past those terrible events. At the popular kids table, Doris sat chatting with Clark by her side. Jane wondered where Elliott was. Now that he'd told his mother about Bev Something, maybe he was free to have his dinner where he'd been staying, one town away. Candace was at their table, too, as well as the elegant woman who'd been another one of Brian Pike's—what word to use—victims or lovers?

The married lady sat with her friends, joining in the conversation. Mike presided at the biker table, and when raucous laughter erupted, he didn't squelch it.

Evangeline entered the dining room, trailed by Maurice. She didn't look bad for someone who in the last twenty-four hours had been drunk, scared out of her wits, and soaked to the skin, and then had an extended crying jag at the memorial service.

As Evangeline came to the table, Jane greeted her. "I'm so glad to see you looking so well."

"Ugh," she said, putting a hand on Jane's shoulder. "Let's never speak of last night again."

Jane thought they would speak of it again. She had a lot of questions but would wait for a more appropriate time and place.

At the end of the meal, Jane left. Although it was still cool, the sky had completely cleared. She headed across the quad toward Regina Campbell's apartment.

Then she heard them. Again. The footsteps. Damn. The sky was still light and the quad was full of people wandering back to their units from dinner.

"Candace," Jane called, "is that you?" But then she saw Candace approaching from the other direction.

They stopped when they met on the walk.

"I saw you follow him last night." Candace kept her voice low. "From my apartment window I saw him. I saw you on your balcony, and then I saw you come out of your foyer door and walk onto the golf course. Did you figure out who the man in black is?"

"No. I got halfway across the golf course, realized what I was doing was idiotic and unsafe, and turned around."

"I didn't see you come back."

"It all took a while." Jane didn't elaborate.

Candace fidgeted, pressing the toe of her tennis shoe into the sidewalk. "But did you follow him long enough to learn anything?"

Jane thought for a moment. "Not much we hadn't figured out already. He's sure-footed. He knows his way around the golf course. He came prepared. He had a flashlight."

"Young or old?"

"He moves well, but he's not young, I think."

"Ooh, I have an idea." Candace bounced on the balls of both feet. "I eliminated that orderly from long-term care on account of his walk. That means we'd recognize the walk of the man on the golf course if we saw it again. So all we have to do is follow all the men in the community until we see the one who walks the right way. You know, like what we saw."

"Candace, I told you, I stopped following the man because it was too dangerous. What if he's the killer?"

But Candace was getting more excited. "We're only looking for tall, thin, older men. We'll just hang out in the quad or the parking lot. Sooner or later, they'll all come by and we'll walk behind them, studying their walks. As we do it, we'll check each one off the list. It will be perfectly safe."

"Didn't you hear what I said? It's too dangerous." Jane tried a different tack. "It would take forever. Even if we agree it was someone coming from the complex, it could be a resident, or an employee, or even a visitor like Elliott Milner."

"Elliott is short and fat and middle-aged."

"I meant someone who is also a visitor, not

someone who is also short and fat. Surely you see there are too many possibilities."

"I'm gonna do it. Just promise me that when I find him, you'll also check him out. And if you agree with me that it's him, you'll be the one to tell the police."

Jane put a hand on Candace's forearm. "Please, don't."

But Candace pulled away and hurried off in the opposite direction.

Jane rapped on the door to Regina's apartment. No answer. She put her ear to the door. Running water. The scrape of a metal pan across a stainless steel sink. Definitely, there was someone inside. She rapped again.

"Just a sec—oh, it's you. I was just going out." Regina was dressed in yoga pants and a T-shirt. It didn't look as if she was going anywhere.

"This will only take a minute." Jane pushed through the doorway before Regina could protest.

The apartment was furnished in the same generic, model-apartment manner as the guest unit Jane was staying in. Although Regina had been there for months, there were few signs of her personality—no family photos or knickknacks on the shelves. A dozen or so books stood on the sideboard, including *The Great Gatsby*.

"I suppose there is no chance of you leaving me alone until I tell you what you want to know." Regina looked unhappy.

Jane indicated the round table in the dining area. "May we sit down?"

Regina nodded grudgingly and took a chair.

"I've come to ask you about Mary Finnerty. I heard you reading to her at the long-term care facility yesterday. What's your relationship?"

"I do it to be nice. It's a volunteer thing." Regina folded her arms across her chest and leaned back in her chair, away from Jane.

"Do you read to anyone else in long-term care?" Jane waited until Regina shook her head. "She means something to you."

"You're friendly with that detective," Regina finally said. "I saw you follow him out of the memorial service today. Have you told him you heard me reading to Mary?"

"Not yet. I know about Watertown, the convent . . ." She let the last words hang, hoping Regina would think she could fill in the blanks.

Jane waited a full minute. Regina stared at her and said nothing. *That didn't work.* Jane let out a long breath and consciously relaxed her shoulders. She reached across the table and put her hands on Regina's strong arms. Regina didn't pull away. Her features softened. Her mouth twitched. She was dying to tell someone. "Regina, whatever it is, talk to me."

Regina let out a great sigh. Then she talked. "The woman in the long-term care facility is my great-aunt." A tear ran down her cheek and dropped onto the gleaming surface of the dining table.

Jane got up and went into the powder room— easy to find because Regina's apartment was an Emerson, just like her own. She grabbed a box of tissues, returned, and handed it to Regina, who blew her nose.

"Thanks. Mary Finnerty's real name is Violet Germaine. She's my grandmother's sister. They didn't speak. I didn't even know Violet existed until my grandmother . . ." Regina blew her nose again, harder this time. Tears cascaded down her cheeks.

"They didn't speak because your grandmother couldn't forgive Violet, Sister Mary Martha, for leaving the convent," Jane suggested.

Regina nodded miserably. She grabbed another tissue and dabbed her eyes. "I was raised by my grandmother. It was just the two of us. I don't know who my dad is. There's not even a father's name on my birth certificate. My mother died of alcohol poisoning when I was eight. My memory of her is hazy. Even before she died, she left me at my gran's a lot when she was drinking. Ironic, isn't it? My gran couldn't forgive her sister for leaving the convent, but she doted on my mother, who did things so much worse.

"Gran died two years ago." She gave up trying to stop the tears. "Of course, she was old. I knew she was old. But she was so strong. I thought she'd last forever. She had a stroke at the supermarket and just died right there, on the spot.

"I thought I was alone in the world, but then I remembered something from my childhood. An argument, a screaming match between my mother and Gran. Fights weren't unusual, especially when my mother was drinking. But you know how sometimes when you're a kid, you can tell things are important even though you don't understand them, and you remember them vividly? They're stored away for when you can make sense of them, and then you bring them out."

Jane nodded. She had some memories like that.

"They were fighting because my mother had gone to Gran's sister, her Aunt Violet, and asked for money. Gran was furious. After Gran died, I got curious. In her address book, I found an address in East Watertown with no name above it. I knew it had to be her sister. I went there. It was a huge two-family house on a beautiful street.

"As a realtor, it was easy for me to find the deed to the house. The house had been sold five years earlier by Violet Germaine. Then Violet seemed to disappear. She hadn't bought any property to replace the house. I searched through elderly housing, nothing. I checked death certificates. But then I found the most unexpected thing. A marriage license. I found it online at the Secretary of State's office in Maryland. Violet Germaine and William Finnerty. Who gets married for the first time ever in her seventies? Once I had the groom's name, and the time frame when they would have purchased, it was easy to track them here. When the agent's job opened up, I grabbed it."

"When you found her, was your great-aunt able to give you any of the answers you were looking for?"

Regina snuffled and shook her head. "When I got here, it was too late. Aunt Violet was too far advanced into Alzheimer's. The picture I'd had of spending time talking about what Gran was like as a child was never going to happen. So I began reading to Violet whenever I could, coaxing out what memories I could."

"Why didn't you tell people Mary is your aunt?"

"When I came here, I fully intended to tell people about my relationship with Aunt Violet. But Bill Finnerty scared me. When I saw how much younger he was, and heard everybody calling my aunt 'Mary' instead of 'Violet,' I knew something was terribly wrong. I didn't know what he was playing at."

"Did he know you were suspicious of him?"

"He knew I read to Mary. He said he was grateful. But I saw him looking at me curiously a few times. I figured he'd checked into my background the same way I'd checked into his. It wouldn't be hard for him to discover I'm related to Violet Germaine."

"You were a threat to him."

"I was afraid of him."

"Afraid enough to kill him?"

"No! I swear. I never confronted him. I stayed out of his way."

"With Pike dead, what were you afraid of? Why didn't you come forward after he was killed?"

She dropped her head. "I will, for sure. Once the murderer's caught. Until then I'm worried I'll become the prime suspect in his death. With Pike dead, I'm my aunt's only living heir. There's one more thing you don't know. My great aunt is very rich."

Rich! "How did an ex-nun school teacher become rich, much less very rich?"

Regina smiled. "My aunt won the Massachusetts

State lottery in the 1980s. She was one of the first winners."

If this was true, it was amazing. It also meant that Violet Germaine could, in all probability, spend the rest of her days in Walden Spring. "Is that why Pike married her, for her money?"

"It's why I was afraid of him. He had a lot to lose if I came forward." Regina hesitated. "Will you be telling the police all of this?"

· "No," Jane said, borrowing a page from Alvarez's book. "You're going to tell them, and I advise doing it soon. The state police are focused on the murder now, but they'll only travel up so many dead ends before they turn their attention to Mary. They'll ask the employees at long-term care if anyone shows a particular interest in her. It will be much better if you go to the police before they come to you."

Chapter Twenty-four

Jane stayed with Regina until she calmed down, then headed back to her apartment. It was fully dark by then, and there were few people on the walks. In the quad, once again, she heard the footsteps. This time, she whirled around and caught him.

"You! Why have you been following me?"

"I could ask the same of you," Mike Witkowski answered. "You followed me onto the golf course last night. And, I've heard through the grapevine, you saw me out there the night of the murder."

"You're the man in black." Of course he was. He always dressed in black from head to toe. But that didn't explain why he walked across the golf course every night.

"Yes, I'm the guy. Now that I've confirmed it, we need to talk." He led her to one of the benches that lined the quad. "What are you going to do about it?"

"Have you told the police you were out on the golf course the night Bill was murdered?"

He had the good sense to look embarrassed. "No."

"You should. I've already said I saw a man walking on the golf course the night of the murder. Another witness saw you, too."

"Telling them would bring up all kinds of useless complications. The state cops have already had me in for a long talk about my prior relationship with Pike."

"That's why you have to tell. It will look terrible if they figure it out on their own."

"As I explained to Detective Fitz when he brought me in for my interview, I didn't hate Brian Pike. When he arrested me, we were both young men, though I'm more than ten years older than he was. He was walking a beat. I was in business as a middleman, receiving stolen goods. He caught me in the act. He sent me away."

Mike leaned back and cracked his knuckles. "Getting arrested was the best thing that ever happened to me. When I got out, I walked the straight and narrow. Gave up drinkin', druggin', and whorin'. I found a good woman and started a garage, Witkowski Collision Repair. It's still in Waltham. My two boys run it now.

"Then my Carrie Ann got Parkinson's. We figured it out early, thank you God, but I knew eventually the day would come when I couldn't care for her. I bought into Walden Spring. We were just old enough to get in. I cared for her at home, in our unit, for four years, and she spent three more at the long-term care. Pike and Mary arrived the last year Carrie Ann was alive. She died five years ago last spring."

"Did you recognize Pike right away? Did he recognize you?"

"I didn't recognize him when he first came here. You'd think I would, the guy who pinched me, but it was the last place I expected to see him and he was using a fake name. Last place he expected to see me, too. And, of course, we were both a lot older."

"And then at some point, each of you realized—"

"Yep, though I never said a word to him directly about it, and neither did he."

"Then why the hostility? Did he try to blackmail you? Threaten you in any way?" *The way he had Karl and Paul.*

Mike shook his head. "Nothing like that. You see, whatever he thought he had on me, I had worse on him. At least I was who I said I was. He couldn't risk exposure. From the time he arrived, I didn't like the con he was running here, I didn't like the way he bullied Peavey and the effect that had on the community, on the friends and neighbors I'd lived with for years. I didn't like what he was doing to Doris, and I couldn't stand his little clique. So we started picking on each other—nothing big, pranks more like it—and it escalated.

"The funny thing is, over time, I changed my mind. To see him with Mary, the way he cared for her, it made me respect him, against all my prejudices. Everybody has some good and some bad in them. I, more than anybody, know that. By the

time I came to that conclusion, the feud was established. We gave everybody a reason to get their
blood moving, I expect."

"So your pranks were for the good of the community?"

He grinned. "I really did think they were, for
the most part. Until the end, when it got out of
hand."

"You never said why you walk the golf course
every night."

Mike stood up from the bench. "Come with me,"
he said. "There's someone I want you to meet."

Jane walked with Mike through the archway past
the entrance to Paul Peavey's office and into the
parking lot. She hadn't been the slightest bit fearful up to that point, talking to Mike in the very
public quad while people had their sliding doors
open on the balconies above. But now, she hesitated. Mike had confirmed he was a convicted
felon who had been arrested by Brian Pike, and he
was on the golf course the night of the murder.
The police were looking at him closely as a suspect. Perhaps she "knew too much" and he was
going to dump her body in the woods. But the
story Mike told rang true. Alvarez had confirmed
he hadn't been arrested since the first time. He'd
built a successful, legitimate business. And he
clearly had cared deeply for his late wife.

Mike went over to his motorcycle, leaned into
Leon's sidecar, and pulled out a helmet. He rested
the helmet on the motorcycle seat, reached back in,

and pulled out a second one. "C'mon," he called as she dawdled under the arch. "Live a little."

What to do? Mike stood next to the motorcycle, his smile visible under the sodium lights of the parking lot. Jane pulled her phone out of her bag and texted Helen.

Taking a motorcycle ride with Mike Witkowski.

Then she climbed into the sidecar, strapped on the helmet, and gave Mike the thumbs up.

As they whooshed down Walden Spring's long drive, she felt an exhilarating freedom—and every bump in the road. Her respect for Leon and his oxygen tank climbed. Her spine rattled, and she dreaded climbing out of the thing, which she was sure would be a graceless affair.

At the bottom of the drive, Mike took a right on the road into town, and a few rump-whacking, jaw-jarring minutes later they pulled up in front of a small, white Cape Cod house with a neat front lawn. The backyard of the house, if Jane wasn't mistaken, bordered on the line of trees on the far side of the Walden Spring golf course.

Mike came around and gave Jane a hand getting out, which was a good thing or she might have been there still. The lights were on in every downstairs room of the house, and as they walked up the drive Jane heard dishes being washed, the sound drifting through an open window. Mike mounted the stairs to the kitchen door, opened it for Jane and said, "C'mon in."

The woman at the kitchen sink turned, wiped

her hands on a dish towel, and put her cheek up to Mike to be kissed. "Elaine," Mike said, "this is Jane, a friend from Walden Spring."

Elaine reached out and took Jane's hand. "Nice to meet you." She was a good deal younger than Mike, late forties perhaps. Her long blond hair was laced with a gray, and the skin around her eyes and on her brow was wrinkled. Her smile was warm, but she looked as if she hadn't had an easy life. "So nice to meet one of Mike's female friends. It's usually 'the boys,' as I call them," she said. "We have a little iced tea this time of night. Will you join us?"

"I'd like that." Jane was deeply curious. Who was this woman to Mike?

"I'll just go let the kids know I'm here." Mike went through the kitchen doorway toward the sounds of a TV or video game.

"Sit down, sit down." Elaine motioned to the kitchen table. She fixed three glasses of tea.

"How did you meet Mike?" Jane asked her.

"My knight in shining armor?" Elaine put the glasses on the table and took the seat next to Jane. "My boys, Kyle and Scott, they're thirteen and fourteen. They were going over to the golf course and getting into all kinds of trouble. Their dad, he's not in the picture, but he's not totally out, either, which would actually be better, and my boys, since they've been teenagers . . . They don't listen like they used to, you know what I mean?"

Jane nodded. "I know exactly what you mean. I brought up my son by myself, with a father who was gone but who wouldn't go away."

Elaine smiled. "So you understand. Last spring, Mike caught the two of them over on the course trying to steal a golf cart. He gave them the business, then hauled them over here and made them apologize to me for being such hooligans. Afterward we got to talking about kids. Mike had raised two boys who turned out okay. He took an interest and started coming by regular. Far more regular than their father. And then—"

Mike came back into the room and sat down at the table. "Getting acquainted?"

"I was telling Jane how we met. How do you two know each other?"

Mike rolled his shoulders. "Walden Spring. Sooner or later everybody knows everybody."

"That awful murder," Elaine said. "So scary. You know it wasn't too far from here. Have they caught anybody yet?"

Mike looked at Jane. She suspected he hadn't said anything to Elaine about his connection to Pike or the state police's recent interest in him. "Not as yet," he said.

One of the boys drifted into the kitchen. He walked past the grown-ups, threw open the refrigerator, and stared into it with a posture Jane remembered well, as if waiting for inspiration to strike.

"Nothing new is going to materialize in there," Elaine said. "Take something, or don't and close the door. If you don't care about the electric bill, at least care about the planet."

"If you don't care about the planet, care about the electric bill," Mike countered. "Come say hello to Mrs. Darrowfield."

The boy closed the door and approached the table. "Hi," he said, "I'm Kyle."

"Nice to meet you."

The other boy came in and introduced himself as well. They were both gangly adolescents, with big feet and Adam's apples. Mike picked a deck of cards off the kitchen hutch and dealt blackjack to the boys. The kids were soon joking with each other and with Mike, teasing the one who guessed wrong. "Look, Mom, twenty-one exactly!" Kyle crowed.

It was a nice domestic scene. Jane could see why Elaine valued Mike and his interactions with the boys. They probably needed a man in their lives, just like Bridget Finnerty's kids needed Alvarez. Jane said a silent thank you to all those men willing to raise other men's children. Would it have made a difference if she'd found one for her son?

Jane stayed for a spirited five-handed game of poker. Mike took them all for their piles of chips, though Kyle hung in to the bitter end. After asking the boys to clean up, Mike rose and gestured to Jane. "C'mon, I'll take you home."

She gave Elaine a hug. "It was lovely to meet you."

"You, too. Come again. You're a welcome change from Mike's usual friends."

"Hey!" Mike laughed, and Elaine did, too.

As they walked out down the drive, Jane asked, "So the walks on the golf course at night?"

"Well, we're not married. And those are two impressionable boys."

"So you sneak into the house after they're in bed?"

"And out again before daybreak."

"Do you really think you're fooling anyone?"

"I don't. But she does, and it's important to her."

"You skipped the two nights after the body was found."

"It seemed like the prudent thing to do."

"You probably know the sprinkler schedule better than anybody." *Except Paul Peavey.*

Mike laughed. "I bet I do. It is a strange thing about the sprinklers."

"What will happen, with you and Elaine?" Jane asked.

"I dunno. All my money's tied up at Walden Spring, and you don't get out of those things so easily, especially after the kind of care they gave to Carrie Ann." He waved in a gesture that took in the whole house behind them. "Who knew I'd be starting again at this time in my life? Who knew I'd want to?"

Who, indeed? Mike, older than Jane, taking on a lover and a pair of teenagers in the bargain. It seemed to suit him. "One more thing," she asked. "Did you see anyone else on the golf course the night Brian Pike was murdered?"

Mike shook his head. "Absolutely no one."

Chapter Twenty-five

Jane returned to the apartment, kicked off her shoes, and dropped into her spot on the couch. Truly an exhausting day after a long, exhausting night. She wasn't hopeful but couldn't help herself. She glanced at her cell phone to see if Harry had called.

There was a text message from Helen.

You're taking a what with who?
Jane texted back: **Long story. Talk tomorrow.**

And there were twenty-three phone messages. All from Candace.

Jane had turned her ringer off at the memorial service that afternoon. Then, after she'd texted Helen, she'd dropped the phone into her bag and forgotten about it.

"Hi, Jane! It's Candace. I'm in the parking lot. It's not Calvin Smith!"

"Hi Jane! It's Candace. It's not Ben Furness. Darn. I thought he was a good bet."

"Jane, Candace here. Not Neil McGregor. Believe it or not, he's *too* tall."

"Jane, Candace. I've switched over to the quad. It's not Roland Hornsby."

And so on. For nineteen more messages. Jane almost deleted the rest without listening, but something propelled her. There was a sort of hypnotic fascination with queuing up the message, pressing play, pressing delete. Repeat.

When the last message came in, she was barely listening, more fascinated by the process than the content. "Jane. It's me. I'm about to give up. It's past dark. Wait, hold on a minute, here's one last possibility. You won't believe it. It's Maurice." There were a few seconds of dead air. Jane's heart rate climbed. "I don't think he's the man on the golf course," Candace said. "But it's the weirdest thing. He's headed to the old swimming pool. Why would he go there at this time of night? I'm following him. Come as soon as you get this. I'm not sure what to say when I catch up to him. I'll try to wait for you. Hurry!"

Jane stared at the time stamp. Eighteen minutes ago. And it was the last call to come in. *Candace, what have you done?* Jane dialed right back. *Pick up, pick up.* Nothing.

Jane dashed out of the apartment and rushed toward the old swimming pool, jogging as fast as she could on the grass. The fake gaslights lit the quad and the driveway to long-term care, but once she turned off the drive and got far enough from the buildings, she could barely see. Off to her left, the long-term care facility was lit up like a jack-o'-lantern, but where she was going was darkness. She stopped and pulled her phone from her pocket. She turned on the flashlight app. She dialed Candace as she jogged toward the woods. No answer.

Jane slowed as she came over the hill, breathing hard. The garden in the woods that surrounded the old pool opened up in front of her. She couldn't make out anything else. If the pool was beautiful in the daylight, it was terrifying at night.

Jane turned off the phone flashlight, stood still, and listened. A rustling. On the other side of the pool. An animal. But was it the human kind?

She dialed Candace's number. Where was she? After a few seconds, a mechanized version of "Send in the Clowns" rose up out of the bottom of the pool. Candace's ringtone, no doubt. No answer. Jane walked cautiously to the edge.

"Candace!" she hissed, her fear rising, heart beating even faster. "Candace!"

She dialed, and the sad little song played again. Then Jane spotted it. A pale blue glow on top of the thin layer of leaves in the hole. She put the flashlight back on and aimed it toward the blue light.

Candace was on her back in the deep end. Her eyes open, lifeless. Beside her was a heavy flashlight, the old-fashioned kind. "Candace!" Jane cried out before she could stop herself. "Oh, Candace!"

A sound. A definite rustling. Not from the other side of the pool, but from her side and close by.

Jane pressed 911.

"Concord Police Department. What is your emergency?"

Maurice loomed out the darkness. He swung something back over his head.

"Help! I'm at Walden Spring—"

Something struck Jane on the shoulder. Her hand jumped, and the phone got loose and clattered to the bottom of the pool.

Jane ran. She skittered along the crumbling side of the pool. She had a head start, but she could hear Maurice's footsteps gaining on her. She rounded the corner at the deep end. The statue of Diana in her temple loomed ahead. Jane had seconds to make a decision. She could veer off into the bamboo maze, but in the darkness the odds of running into something, getting hurt, or being trapped were too high.

She ran toward the headless statue of Diana, the huntress. Bits of stone came loose from the side of the pool wall and fell into it. Behind her, Maurice cursed her for interfering, for ever being born. "Why couldn't you mind your own business!"

They were at the deepest end of the empty pool, a twenty-foot drop even the leaves wouldn't cushion. It wouldn't kill her—something else, something worse must have happened to Candace—but the fall might injure her and would certainly trap her. And the snakes! Jane shivered as she ran. The statue was straight ahead. She'd have to go around it, over it, or through it. How? If she couldn't get around the statue, Maurice would have her cornered.

At the last minute Jane made her decision and ran right at Diana.

"Why couldn't you mind your own business, you silly cow!" Maurice yelled, close behind her.

Just before she collided with Diana, Jane reached out, put her hands around Diana's neck, and swung her body in an arc out over the pool with all the strength she had. Her feet left the ground. Her shoulders screamed from the stress. The statue rocked in its pedestal, and for a second she thought both she and Diana would tumble into the waterless pool. She held on, barely, rotating around. Her feet found the pool wall on the other side of Diana. She let go. Pain shot from her ankles to her knees. She regained her balance and ran on.

Maurice was still behind her. He had the same decision to make. Run around Diana and her temple, or do what Jane had done. She heard the statue rock again. He'd come the way she had.

Crack! The sound was like a thunderbolt as the statue broke off its pedestal. Maurice shrieked as he fell down, down into the darkness. There was a thump at the bottom of the pool and then the sound of rock hitting rock. Maurice screamed again. And again. And again.

Jane stopped running when she realized his screams had changed. They weren't screams of surprise, but of agony. Maurice was in the bottom of the pool, badly hurt.

She had to get help for Maurice and maybe for Candace, though Jane was sure there was little hope for her. Was help on the way? Jane hadn't been able to tell the emergency operator anything beyond "Walden Spring." Did she take Jane seriously? And even if they did, could they figure out where she was? Walden Spring had acres and acres.

Jane took off back through the woods toward the path to the long-term care facility. It was the closest building, staffed at night. It had phones.

Her lungs burned and her heart hammered. She veered from the path and headed straight for the building, a shorter route. She ran on through the trees. It was so dark.

Then *bang!* She heard it the same instant that she felt it. She slid to the ground and into the black.

Chapter Twenty-six

Monday, August 13

J ane woke up in a hospital room. Detective Alvarez, Paul Peavey, and Karl Flagler hovered over her as if she were Dorothy and they were the farmhands in *The Wizard of Oz.*

"There you are," Alvarez said softly when she opened her eyes.

"How did I get here?" Jane asked.

"Your 911 call went through. The dispatcher sent the Concord police and an ambulance to Walden Spring," Alvarez said. "Given there'd been a murder there the week before, the Concord police alerted the state police."

"But all I had time to tell them was that I was at Walden Spring." Jane tried hard to remember. "How did they find me . . . us?"

"There was quite a search. Naturally, because Pike's body was found there, they started on the golf course and worked outward. About dawn they located Maurice and Candace in the old swimming pool. He was conscious when they found him. He claimed he hadn't seen you. They knew the call came from your number. Paul Peavey called me. I verified you weren't at your home in Cambridge, so the search continued. They located you about an hour later. It was Karl who found you."

Jane's eyes stung. "I am so grateful." Karl stepped forward and squeezed her hand. "What happened to me?"

"You ran headlong into a tree," Karl answered. "Hit a big branch square on your forehead and knocked yourself out. I found you crumpled up underneath it."

"Candace?" Jane asked, though she knew the answer.

"Dead," Alvarez confirmed. "I am so sorry."

"Maurice?"

"In this hospital," Alvarez answered. "On another floor with police guards posted outside his door. He shattered both legs when he fell into the empty pool. Jane, he confessed to both murders."

"Why? Why would Maurice have killed Brian Pike—and Candace?"

"Maurice is in love with Evangeline. He knew Evangeline was having an affair with Bill Finnerty. He says he couldn't stand the way Bill Finnerty treated her. On the night of the murder, Bill and Evangeline met on the golf course. Maurice snuck out after her. He says he'd tried to convince Evangeline to break it off, and he wanted to see if she would actually do it. Bill drove up in his golf cart, cool as a cucumber, his clubs still in the back. Apparently Evangeline lost her nerve, or Bill talked her into staying with him. Whatever happened, Maurice didn't like what he heard. He snuck up to the cart, took a club out of the bag, and bashed Bill over the head with it."

"Was Evangeline there when it happened? Did she witness Pike's murder?"

"Maurice claims she'd already left."

"But why kill Candace?" Jane croaked.

"Maurice hid the golf club in the old pool. He grew worried Detective Fitz would eventually have that area searched, and he went to retrieve it. For some reason Candace followed him. I don't think we'll ever know why. He discovered her and killed her with his flashlight. Then he threw her body in the pool."

"I know why Candace followed Maurice," Jane said. "She had a scheme to follow all the tall, skinny men at Walden Spring to identify the man in black who walked the golf course at night by his gait. I tried to talk her out of it. I didn't think she'd really do it. It wasn't even Maurice. She got carried away with the hunt."

"I warned you about playing detective," Alvarez said. "So Candace was the other person who saw the mystery man out on the golf course the night of the murder."

"Yes, she was. She thought because of her medical history she wouldn't be believed." Jane shook her head. A stabbing pain traveled from ear to ear, and a burst of light flashed behind her eyes. "Oooh."

"Easy," Alvarez said.

"The shame of it is, it didn't matter. The man in black had nothing to do with the murder. It's Mike

Witkowski. He has a girlfriend in a house on the other side of the golf course. I learned that after my last conversation with Candace. I never got a chance to tell her."

"It's not your fault," Paul said.

Jane gave them a weak smile because smiling hurt. It was good to have the whole horrible mess behind them, even if the solution didn't feel quite right.

Her eyelids were suddenly heavy. She closed her eyes and drifted back to sleep.

When Jane woke up, sometime in the late afternoon by the look of the sun through the hospital window, there was a large bouquet of roses on the bedside table. Harry sat in the guest chair. "How did you know I was here?" Jane asked.

"Hello, yourself." He laughed. "How are you feeling?"

"Okay, I guess. My head hurts."

"Not surprising. You must have been running full tilt when you hit that branch. There's some swelling in your brain. That's why you were admitted. The reason for all this." His arm swept around to the various monitors she was hooked up to. Equipment she'd barely noticed before. "Don't mess with your brain. It's dangerous. You need to be watched."

"You didn't answer my question."

"When you didn't answer your phone, I went out to Walden Spring to look for you. I was on the way to pound on your door when Peavey saw me pass by his office. He told me you were here."

Harry shifted in the hospital chair. "There's something else you need to know." Harry's luxuriant eyebrows came together over his nose. "Peavey gave me the number of your friend, Detective Alvarez. I called him and introduced myself."

Normally this would have raised Jane's ire. Why was he butting into her life? But in her weakened state, she asked in a calm and open tone, "Why would you do that?" Maybe there was something to be said for a weakened state.

"In law enforcement, it's considered polite, if you come in contact in someone else's investigation, to let them know you're around. I really should have called Detective Fitz, but you seemed to like Detective Alvarez so much better, I figured I'd start there."

Jane was so distracted she barely heard the last bit. "Law enforcement? I thought you worked for a multinational company?"

"I never said that. You assumed, and I didn't correct you. I'm sorry not to have been more forthcoming. I've found, over the years, that a lot of people have trouble seeing beyond the job when I tell them what I do for work."

"You're a cop?"

"No, federal."

"FBI?"

"More of an international focus."

"You're a spy?"

"We don't use that word. And not exactly. Anyway, I'm retired. Now I consult on security for multinational companies, so you weren't entirely wrong. Everything else I told you was true. I did travel too much when my boys were growing up. I was too focused on my job. I'm determined not to make that mistake again."

"Don't apologize. I hope we're going to discover lots of interesting things about each other."

Harry inched his chair closer to the bed. "I'm sorry if you feel like I've rushed you. It's just that I don't want to take it too slow. Who knows how much time we have?"

"Geez, we're not that old."

"No, we're not. But at least one of us seems to have a dangerous job."

When Harry got ready to go, he said, "You get your rest. They'll discharge you in the morning if everything checks out. Do you want me to come help you move your stuff out of Walden Spring?"

"Yes . . . no . . . maybe," Jane said.

"Well, as long as you're sure." Harry kissed her hand and was gone.

Chapter Twenty-seven

Tuesday, August 14

Detective Fitz arrived to take her statement in the morning just as the attendant cleared away Jane's breakfast tray.

"I'm glad you're doing better," he said. "It was foolish chasing a murderer into the woods."

"I didn't know he was a murderer," Jane answered. "Besides, I wasn't chasing Maurice. I was chasing Candace."

"Poor Mrs. Brown." Fitz paused, and then said more sternly. "Nonetheless."

Jane sat up as straight as she was able to in a hospital bed. "You had some questions for me."

He walked her through the night of Candace's murder. When he asked her why she'd picked up Candace's messages so late, she told him about Mike Witkowski and Elaine. There didn't seem to be any harm in it.

When they finished, Fitz thanked her. "And thank

you, too, for telling Regina Campbell to provide the real identity of Mary Finnerty."

"You're welcome, though I'm not sure how instrumental I was. Once Maurice confessed, Regina had nothing to lose by revealing the relationship."

"It all checks out. Violet Germaine married 'William Finnerty' in Maryland a week before they moved to Walden Spring," Fitz said.

"Why didn't the police find that out?"

Fitz pulled his head back into his neck like a turtle. "We would have, I'm sure. Remember we only had half the equation. We didn't know Violet Germaine's real name, and William Finnerty is very common. The marriage took place in another state. Our primary focus was on the homicide."

"Is it true that Violet Germaine is rich?"

"She was the second person ever to win Mass Megabucks. In 1983, she won over a million dollars. As far as we can tell, she continued to teach math at a Cambridge middle school and live modestly. She invested prudently and sold that big house at the top of the market."

"What's her relationship to Brian Pike? Did he marry her for her money?"

Fitz shook his head. "Doesn't look that way. When she taught in Cambridge she was Pike's math teacher. Years later, her school was on his beat and evidently that's how they renewed their friendship. After the accident where the Finnertys were killed, Pike fled to Violet's house. According to the neighbors, he lived there for years, less than a mile from the Cambridge line."

"All that time," Jane mused. "Was the marriage a real one?"

"Apparently, Ms. Campbell's grandmother's issue with Violet, and the reason they never reconciled, was that later in life, Violet had a man living with her. We don't know the exact nature of Violet and Brian's relationship, whether the marriage was real, or the relationship was ever consummated. I suppose now we never will."

"It's remarkable that Brian Pike took care of Violet the way he did."

"The aunt who raised him suffered from Alzheimer's," Fitz told her. "He must have recognized Violet's symptoms and decided to find a place for her. They sold the Watertown house, married, and moved to Walden Spring. He could have left her at any time. In the early days of her confusion, he probably could have walked off with most of her money. But he didn't. He left all he could in her real name and didn't touch it as far as we can tell."

"So Doris was right in her eulogy. Brian Pike wasn't all bad."

Fitz's mouth turned up, but there was sadness in his eyes. "Yes, but mostly he was bad."

Jane thought about the vulnerable women Pike had taken advantage of, the threats he'd held over Paul and Karl. The chaos he'd caused in the community. Yes, mostly he was bad, but not entirely.

"Does all this mean Violet can stay at Walden Spring?"

"That's a question for Paul Peavey, but she does have the money."

That was one happy ending at least. But Jane couldn't shake the feeling she'd had since she'd awoken the day before: Things weren't as tied up as Fitz believed. "I don't think Maurice killed Brian Pike," she said.

"He confessed."

"I know. I just don't think he . . . The way he behaved after Pike's murder wasn't . . ." Clearly the blow to her head was causing her trouble in completing thoughts.

"Mr. Cohen confessed. He had the murder weapon. The sprinklers obliterated the evidence on the golf course. We're not looking at anyone else."

"That's another thing," Jane said. "There's something wrong about the sprinklers." Mike Witkowski's words floated back to her, spoken when he'd dropped her off that night, before she ran out toward the old pool. Before all this happened. "It's a strange thing about the sprinklers," he'd said.

Fitz cut her off. "Mrs. Darrowfield, you've told me Mr. Cohen chased you around the marble pool trying to kill you, or at least harm you. I think, if you reflect on all your adventures, you'll conclude we've got the right man."

Harry drove her back to Walden Spring later that day. She'd been discharged from the hospital with a passel of cautions and restrictions, chief among them, no driving. She asked him to give her some time in the apartment to pack her things and say her good-byes. He didn't argue, though he looked like he wanted to. His mouth was firmly shut, jaw clenched. She could see the effort he put into keeping quiet.

It worried her that he felt he couldn't speak his

mind. If they were going to make it as a couple, they were going to have to learn to disagree more effectively. Or maybe only she was. Harry, after all, had a long and successful marriage, something she couldn't claim.

"I can't wait until you get out of here," Harry said when he kissed her good-bye. "I want you back in your own home and your own kitchen. You can fix me a lovely gourmet meal."

Gourmet meal? What the heck was he talking about? Phyllis's darn Getadate profile. Yes, they would be revealing themselves to each other for some time to come. At least that one could wait until she got home.

As she packed, Jane couldn't shake the unease that had crept up on her at the hospital. The morning Brian Pike's body had been found, Maurice had been his joking, acerbic self. It was Evangeline who had been off-kilter, barely able to hold herself together. Detective Alvarez had said Pike's murder had been a crime of passion. Evangeline was the passionate one. Maurice had only one passion—Evangeline.

But she knew who had chased her around the pool, knew who had ended up at the bottom. And there was still the problem of the sprinklers.

Karl Flagler answered the door to the caretaker's cottage. He smiled when he saw who it was, but there must have been something in Jane's expression. "What's up?" he asked.

"We need to talk. About the sprinklers. Can I come in?"

He raised a quizzical eyebrow and stepped back. "I guess you'd better."

They settled in the cozy living room of the cottage, Jane in the comfy chair she'd occupied in the small hours of Sunday morning. To all appearances it was a congenial visit, but Jane was on a mission. "Karl, the sprinklers are supposed to go off on Monday, Wednesday, and Saturday."

"Yes."

"I took that to mean, and the police took that to mean, Monday, Wednesday, and Saturday evening. But the other night, when I was out on the golf course, the sprinklers came on at one-fifteen a.m., not on Saturday night, but on Sunday morning."

"So?"

"So when everyone around here says the sprinklers go on Monday, Wednesday, and Saturday, what they are actually saying is that they come on overnight, on Tuesday, Thursday, and Sunday, at one-fifteen in the morning."

The smile left Karl's face, but his tone remained polite. "I don't see what you're getting at."

"Brian Pike's body was found Wednesday morning. The sprinklers shouldn't have come on overnight when Pike was killed. Yet, not only did the sprinklers come on, they stayed on, obliterating all the footprints and every other piece of physical evidence at the scene. You turned them on. You threw the manual override. Why?"

Karl didn't deny the accusation. He couldn't. No one else could have done it. He stared down at his hands, fiddling with his father's wedding ring. Finally, he spoke. "Paul left in the middle of that night while I was asleep. It's not an unusual thing for him to do. I get up early and work a long day. He doesn't always wake me to say good-bye. But the night of the murder, something woke me up around three."

"Was it the noise of the murder that woke you?"

"I don't think so. It was a hot night, and we had the air-conditioning on. I'd hate to think that if I'd heard . . ." He faltered. "I could have stopped it.

"You went to investigate."

"Yes. I went out on the front porch and the lights went on. I saw the golf cart. I was annoyed. I thought it was high school joy riders. I walked over and looked more closely and that's when I saw—"

"The body."

Karl gathered himself and continued. "Yes. By then my footprints were all over the green. And so were Paul's. I couldn't take the chance. I turned on the sprinklers."

"You used the computer over there," Jane pointed, "to override the schedule and turn the sprinklers on manually."

"I didn't sleep. After the sunrise, I turned the sprinklers off and walked only as far onto the course as I needed to see the body. I called Paul, and he called the police."

Jane could think of only one reason why Karl might have done what he did. "You were afraid Paul killed him."

Karl turned gray behind his tan, but he stood his ground. "Paul would have had plenty of good reasons, if he had."

"You destroyed physical evidence."

Karl shifted in his chair, looking uncomfortable.

"Do you still think Paul might have done it?" Jane asked.

"No." Karl's voice broke. "And not because Maurice confessed. I could tell the minute I told Paul about the body he knew nothing about it. I'm ashamed now that I ever thought it."

"Have you told Paul what you did? The sprinklers?"

"No. He can never know."

Jane leaned forward. Karl tried to look at her but couldn't. "You must tell Paul," Jane said. "It's too big a secret to keep. The question of the sprinklers will come up in Maurice's trial, if there is one. You may be compelled to testify. Besides, I'm sure Paul already knows what you did. He creeps across that golf course every night. Probably no one knows that sprinkler schedule better than he does. He's been covering for you. He may even think you turned on the sprinklers to cover your tracks because you committed the murder."

Karl was plainly horrified. "Oh, my God."

Jane lifted Karl's strong chin and made him look at her. "Tell Paul now, while things are calm. Given time, this will poison you two as a couple. And then you have to tell Detective Fitz. He won't like it, but it's better that he hears it now and not at Maurice's trial."

Karl nodded that he understood. "Maurice," he said. "Who'd have thought. I never would have pegged him as a killer."

"No one would have," Jane responded. "No one at all."

Chapter Twenty-eight

It was lunchtime when Jane made her way back across the golf course from Karl's cottage. The residents of Walden Spring descended on the clubhouse. Jane joined the throng.

Naturally, she attracted a lot of attention. A wave of commentary followed her wherever she went. When she passed behind the popular kids table, Doris rose and gave her a hug. "Thank you," she whispered.

"I'm so sorry about Candace," Jane said.

"Me too." Doris wiped a tear from her eye. "But I am so glad this is over."

Mike came over and shook her hand. "Now maybe things can get back to normal around here."

Jane sat next to Ethel at the artists and dancers table. Evangeline wasn't there, but everyone else was. Jane had wondered whether most of them would be at Evangeline's apartment, the way the popular girls had gathered at Doris's house after Bill died. But evidently having your companion revealed as a murderer was different from having him revealed as a murderee. All the artists and dancers were present and accounted for.

"I'm surprised to see you here," Ethel said in her foghorn voice. "I thought you would go straight home from the hospital."

Jane smiled. "I've come to pick up my things and say my good-byes."

"It's sure been an interesting time since you arrived," Ethel said, an understatement. "I am absolutely shocked about Maurice."

"Me too," Jane agreed. "I'm so shocked, I think the police have the wrong person."

There was a clatter of forks being put down on the hard surface of the table. Around Jane and Ethel, the table went silent.

"What do you mean?" Ethel demanded, evidently speaking for all of them. "I thought Maurice tried to kill you."

"To be clear, he did chase me around the old swimming pool, wielding a golf club. But I don't think he killed Bill Finnerty. And I'm not sure about Candace, either."

"We heard he confessed," the little dancer objected.

"He did. But I don't think he did it. I'm going to keep after the police until they arrest the right person."

When lunch was over, they all lined up to hug her good-bye. "None of that," Jane said, when Ethel snuffled into her handkerchief. "I'm only fifteen miles down the road. I'll be back."

As she walked across the quad toward her apartment, Jane was surprised to discover she hoped she would be. She pulled her cell out of her pocket and called Harry. "Can you pick me up in an hour?" she asked. "It's time for me to go home."

"On my way," he said.

She said good-bye, hung up, and called Detective Alvarez.

Jane took a canvas shopping bag out of a drawer in the kitchen and placed it on the counter. She loaded it with milk, butter, eggs, coffee—all the food she'd brought to the apartment. It was the last bag to be packed. Her suitcase and a tote bag containing her laptop, books, and assorted paraphernalia propped open the front door. Harry would be there momentarily.

The sound of the elevator chugging followed by the clang of the opening doors echoed in the foyer.

"Come in!" Jane called to Harry from the kitchen area. "I'm in here."

"Hello," Evangeline answered. "I heard you were leaving. I've come to say good-bye."

The Walden Spring grapevine had worked even faster than Jane had expected. "Good-bye, Evangeline," she said. "It's been interesting."

Evangeline came fully into the room, leaving the door open, and stood across the vast granite countertop from Jane. "I heard you think Maurice is innocent. I'm so certain of it, I'm going to hire him the best criminal lawyer I can find." Evangeline spread her hands out on the cold stone. "I didn't expect anyone else to believe in him. He confessed."

"He confessed to protect someone else," Jane said.

Evangeline snapped to attention. "What makes you think that?"

"Because nothing else makes sense. I was there the morning the body was discovered, and I remember. Maurice was as surprised as we all were."

"I hardly think that proves anything." Evangeline caught herself. "I mean, it isn't a legal defense."

"And there's the fact that the seventh hole wasn't a place where Bill Finnerty met up with the guys. It was a trysting spot, where he held his famous picnics under the stars."

"Which doesn't mean Maurice didn't sneak up on Bill there. I mean, playing devil's advocate."

"I suppose not. Because the sprinklers were on for hours, we'll never be sure."

Evangeline shifted from one foot to the other. "I was told Maurice attacked you out by the old pool. That makes you a witness."

"It's true he chased me, and I have no doubt he intended to harm me, once he realized I'd seen Candace's body. He knew I'd figure out who had killed her. But I didn't see him kill Candace."

"He killed her." Evangeline didn't sound like someone invested in proving Maurice's innocence.

It didn't surprise Jane. The ideas that had swirled in her hurting head since she'd heard about Maurice's confession had gelled into an unpretty picture. "I don't think he did. I think that after the scene at the memorial service, Maurice confronted you with what he'd figured out. You confessed. You told him everything that had happened."

"Which was what?" Evangeline demanded.

"Which was the man you knew as Bill Finnerty took you out to the golf course to tell you the affair was over. He had a habit of only keeping his side-pieces, or should I say side-sidepieces, for a few months at a time. You, however, were having none of it. You pretended to accept what he said, but you took a golf club from his bag, snuck up behind him when his back was turned, hit him, and kept hitting."

"Ridiculous," Evangeline said. "And even if it were true, you could never prove it."

"You gave Maurice enough detail for his confession to the police to hold up. You told him you'd hidden the golf club in the old pool, a special place for you. As the investigation dragged on, and the police didn't arrest Mike Witkowski as you'd hoped, you were fearful they would broaden their search for the murder weapon."

Across the countertop, Evangeline glowered. But she didn't leave, which an innocent person would have done.

Jane pressed on. "Candace followed Maurice from the quad. You spotted her from your balcony and you followed, too. Maurice had a heavy flashlight. So did you. When he was down in the pool retrieving the golf club, he heard her up above. He shone his flashlight on her, but you were the one, up top, who bashed her in the head with yours and pushed her over the edge.

"That's when you spotted my little phone light and hid. Maurice was out of the pool with the golf club by then. He saw me see Candace and heard me call 911. He came after me while you ran away."

"That's absurd!" Bright red dots shown on each of Evangeline's cheeks. "I have never heard such a pack of wild imaginings and lies."

"I saw you there," Jane said. It was a stab in a very dark night. She had heard something besides Maurice but had seen nothing.

"You couldn't have," Evangeline shrieked. "And even if you did, so what? No jury will take the word of an old woman who saw something moving in the night."

Jane looked her in the eye. "Maybe not. But they'll believe this." Jane reached into her pocketbook and laid her white keycard on the countertop. "This keycard tracks every time you use it. Yours will show that you, not Maurice, returned to your building and your unit in the wee hours of the morning Brian Pike was killed, after you'd murdered him, and after you'd gone all the way out to the old pool to hide the golf club. And it will show you letting yourself in after Maurice was in the bottom of the pool with two broken legs and I was lying unconscious in the woods on the night you killed Candace."

Evangeline howled. She lunged across the counter and managed to grab hold of Jane's blouse with one hand. Jane twisted away. As Evangeline came around the kitchen island, Jane escaped the other way. As Jane ran out the apartment door, she heard Evangeline raging behind her. "You ruined it all! Everything terrible started the day you came here!"

"Maurice isn't here to take the blame for you

this time," Jane called back over her shoulder. She ran for the stairwell and down the stairs, Evangeline's footfalls clattering behind her. Was she gaining? Jane wished she were her younger self. She wished she could take the stairs two at time. She wished she could let go of the railing like she was certain of her balance. Fortunately, Evangeline was dealing with all the same issues. It was like one of those slow speed car chases you saw on TV. Which was a good thing, because Jane was sure Evangeline would have no compunction about pushing her down the concrete steps if she caught her.

At last, Jane reached the ground floor and burst through the fire door into the foyer. "Help me! Help me!" She kept going, out the glass door into the quad, yelling at the top of her lungs, headed along the path toward Peavey's office.

Then, miracle of miracles, Harry came through the archway, walking casually and talking to Detective Alvarez.

"Harry!" Jane yelled. "Help, Evangeline—" Jane didn't dare look back. She reached Harry and fell into his arms. Alvarez kept moving, catching Evangeline. He didn't let her go.

Chapter Twenty-nine

Detective Alvarez visited Jane at her home in Cambridge the next morning. She offered him coffee, which he declined. Her headache had gone away, but her shins were murderously painful from her run down the stairs. Walking gingerly, she brought him to meet with her in her office, so much more professional than the kitchen table.

"Has Maurice changed his story about what happened to Brian Pike?" she asked.

Alvarez shook his head.

"And Candace's murder?"

"Who's to say what happened out there? If they go to trial, Evangeline and Maurice's attorneys will certainly point the finger at one another in an attempt to create reasonable doubt. You'll be an important witness, but you got there after the fact. You didn't really see Evangeline, did you?"

Jane shook her head. "There were two people

out there that night. I am certain of it, but I couldn't identify anyone beyond Maurice, no."

"The best thing would be if Maurice took a plea deal for assaulting you and testified against Evangeline for the murders," Alvarez said.

"I doubt that will happen. What about the keycard?"

"Mrs. Murray will say Maurice used her card to enter her apartment on the night of the murder. Plenty of people will corroborate he was there all the time."

"It will be harder to explain her entry on the night of Candace's murder."

"It will be. The DA can be pretty persuasive. She'll help Maurice understand he's being played for the fool." Alvarez smiled. "Cheer up. She's good at her job. Like you are."

Chapter Thirty

Tuesday, August 21

The door to Candace's apartment was open. Inside a young woman with a wild mane of chocolate brown hair packed a box. As Paul Peavey had told Jane, Candace's daughter had come to clear out her mother's place. The pictures were down off the walls, and some of the kitchen items were in boxes. The woman looked up and saw her.

"Hello."

"I'm Jane Darrowfield, a friend of your mother's."

The woman straightened up and grasped her hand. "Dina Vincent. You're the one who was hurt when Mom was . . . died."

"I was. I'm so sorry about your mother. I liked her."

Dina looked around the little apartment. "I need to get this place sold as soon as possible," she explained. "I can't afford the fees, even without the food and stuff. That nice realtor told me she'd help me stage it once Mom's junk is cleaned out and the estate stuff seen to."

"Your mother was so happy to be reunited with you," Jane said. "She told me you and your daughters were the best thing in her life."

Dina blinked back tears. "I miss her so much. If you'd told me twenty years ago, or fifteen, I would miss her, I would have said you were as crazy as she was."

"Her illness must have made your life difficult."

Dina nodded while keeping up the sorting and boxing. Jane joined in, pulling items out of cupboard and drawers.

"My childhood was a horror show," Dina said. "My dad couldn't take her illness. He left, and I was alone with a mentally ill mother. A woman who went through cycles of hearing voices telling her not to feed me or not to let me go to school. I was terrified of her. I hated her. Finally the state took me away and put me in foster care. I thought that was the end of me and my mother."

Dina gestured to the coffeemaker on the counter. Jane nodded that she'd take a cup. Candace's half-dozen mismatched mugs sat next to the pot, ready to be packed. That homely collection hurt Jane's heart. Candace had never had all the possessions the rest of them were now so desperately trying to get rid of. She'd never had a place, never found a home, until Walden Spring, only to be murdered here.

"Thank you for helping me," Dina said.

With their steaming cups of coffee in hand, Dina and Jane settled on the couch covered with a colorful quilt.

"Sometime after you were put in foster care, you and your mother got back in touch," Jane said.

"Ten years ago she reached out to me. I was reluctant at first. She'd hurt me so badly. By then I was old enough to understand she couldn't help her illness. But I wasn't sure I wanted to be put in a position where I could be hurt again. But she kept getting in touch. She was so much better. They said she was in remission. She felt awful about everything that had happened, even though it wasn't really her fault. So our second act began."

Tears streamed down Dina's face, but she continued. "You should have seen her with my daughters. They adored her, and she gave them everything she was never able to give me when I was small. We talked every day on the phone."

"Dina, I am so sorry."

"Mom told me about helping you with your search for the murderer. She was so excited, so into it. The day she was killed, she even told me about her plan to follow all the tall men at Walden Spring. I didn't say a word to stop her. I was happy she was feeling useful. I figured there were so many people here. The odds of anything happening were so small. It never occurred to me that it was dangerous."

"Me either," Jane said. "I asked her not to do it, but I should have tried harder to dissuade her." Jane moved next to Dina on the saggy, old couch and took her in her arms. Dina laid her head on Jane's shoulder and wept.

"I wouldn't wish the first twenty years of my life on anyone," Dina cried. "But I wouldn't trade the last ten with my mother for anything."

Word had spread that Jane was at Walden Spring, and a small group gathered under the archway outside Paul Peavey's office to say good-bye: Karl Flagler, Regina Campbell, Mike Witkowski, and his usual crew.

"I have news," Paul told her. "I've tendered my resignation."

"I'm sorry to hear that. I had the impression you loved your job."

"I love parts of it," Paul said. "But there are other parts of it I'm not so good at, as you well know." He smiled and took Karl's hand. "One of us had to go. Karl loves his job. This makes lots of things less complicated."

"You can finally stop sneaking across the golf course at night," Jane said.

"Among other things."

"I'm leaving, too," Regina said. "Aunt Violet's situation is getting settled. She'll have a legal guardian who'll work with me. I'm going to help Candace's daughter get that unit on the market, and attend to some similar things, and then I'm gone."

"Will you stay in the area?" Jane asked.

"Yes. I'll have my own place, but I'll be nearby to visit my aunt. It's past time to give up on some things," Regina glanced at Karl and Paul. "And I don't mean trying to sell condos at Walden Spring."

"And you?" Jane asked Mike.

"Regina's helping me get my unit ready to sell, too. I'm leaving Walden Spring, but I'm not going far."

"You're a brave man," Jane said. "We should all be so brave as we live these final chapters."

"No use in dying before you actually do," Mike said. He gave a nod to his crew. "We'll escort you down the driveway."

Jane roared out of Walden Spring in Old Reliable, smiling to herself, surrounded by eight motorcycles. How much things had changed. This time, she loved the racket.

Chapter Thirty-one

Monday, September 10

It was after Labor Day before their card games started up again. Helen had been at her family house on the Cape. Phyllis was visiting her daughter in the Berkshires. Only Jane and Irma had remained in Cambridge.

Helen and Jane were setting up the card table in Phyllis's living room when Irma rushed in. "Turn on the TV! Turn on the TV!"

It took a little searching, but there on the local cable access channel was Detective Alvarez interviewing Irma's mother, Minnie.

"Can you tell us what happened to you, Mrs. Brittleson?"

"A man called. He said he was from my bank." And out came the whole horrible tale. Minnie, gently urged on by a kind-voiced Detective Alvarez, told how she had been swindled out of her $9,000 burial money.

"Unbelievable!" When Jane had talked to Minnie, she was too embarrassed to go to the police. Yet here she was, telling her story on television for the entire world to hear. Or at least the regular viewers of Cambridge public access television.

"It's that Detective Alvarez," Irma said. "He came to the house and told us he was a friend of yours, Jane. They have the videotapes from the bank, and he figured out Mom was the victim you described. He slowly convinced her to tell her story. He said she could warn other people like herself so they wouldn't make the same mistake. That's what got her to agree."

"Amazing," Phyllis said.

"But that isn't even the most amazing part," Irma said. "This is the fourth time this program has aired. People have been sending money. Mostly five- and ten-dollar bills in envelopes, I'd guess from people who can barely afford it, but some big checks have come in as well from wealthy local families. Mother's made back all her money and started giving the rest to a charity for indigent seniors. That Detective Alvarez is a saint."

Maybe not a saint, but a good man.

They shuffled the cards and began the game. As the day got later, the air had a touch of fall in it. The days were getting shorter, and the edges of the leaves were tinged with yellow and red.

"I have something to tell you all," Jane said when it was her turn during the News of the Week. "I have a boyfriend!" And then she burst into tears.

"Jane," Irma said, "why are you crying?"

"He wants to take me to San Francisco," Jane sobbed. "To see my son."

"Will you go?" Phyllis asked.

"I don't know," Jane cried. "I don't know what to do."

Helen looked as if she was going to say something, but then changed her mind.

"There's something else," Jane continued. "Phyllis, he was meant for you. He was one of your Internet dates. I've been carrying on since the day of the coffee dates, sneaking around. I feel so awful."

Phyllis started to laugh, then Irma. Helen's shoulders began to shake. Soon Jane was laughing, too, though she had no idea why.

"Oh, honey," Phyllis said. "He was always meant for you. I did it all for you. You seemed at such loose ends. We just want you to be happy."

Jane laughed so hard with relief, she started to cry again.

"And Jane," Irma said. "I am so, so sorry I got you mixed up in that awful murder at Walden Spring."

Jane wiped her eyes. "Don't be sorry," she said. "It's the best thing that's happened to me in ages."

Wednesday, October 24

The big plane lifted off from Logan Airport, headed to San Francisco. Jane and Harry were in first class. Harry had said he had enough frequent flyer miles for a lifetime.

Once they leveled off and the engine noise died down, Harry leaned over to her. "I have three days of meetings. That will leave you plenty of time to do whatever you want to do. Or do nothing at all."

Jane's son's address was in her pocketbook,

safely stowed above them. Harry had offered to get the address for her. It wasn't easy to tell someone, even someone you might love, that you were a failure at the one thing in your life that mattered most to you. But Harry had taken it in his stride. He was a kind and supportive man. A wonderful man.

Jane reminded herself about Regina Campbell, who'd wanted a family connection so badly she'd tracked Violet Germaine to Walden Spring. And Dina, Candace's daughter, who wouldn't trade away twenty years of hell if it meant she'd lose the last ten years with her mother. And the relationship between Doris and Elliott Milner, which had dramatically changed for the better after Brian Pike's murder. Anything was possible.

"Thanks." Jane gave Harry's hand a squeeze.

He squeezed back. As far as Jane knew, there were no longer any secrets between them. Harry had listened to her stories with the same respect she'd shown when listening to his. He'd been understanding about all of it. He'd even gotten over her not being a gourmet cook.

Jane leaned back in her seat and closed her eyes. The future wasn't at all certain, which seemed strange at her time of life. But then, when had it ever been?

Acknowledgments

Jane Darrowfield has lived in my imagination for a long time.

Thank you to my writers group, Mark Ammons, Kat Fast, Cheryl Marceau, and Leslie Wheeler for midwifing her with me. Your comments on the manuscript, and more important your friendship, are worth more than you can know.

Thank you to my friend, author Lucy Burdette, for her early-on advice about golf courses (so early on she probably doesn't remember it) and her later advice about the best golf clubs to kill people with. As I told her, "I love that I know exactly the right person to answer this question."

Thanks to my Wicked Cozys: Maddie Day, Jessica Ellicott, Sherry Harris, Julia Henry, and Liz Mugavero. Once again, I could not have made it through this manuscript without your love and support. Thanks especially to Sherry Harris, who edited the manuscript and caught a big, embarrassing error I had somehow missed.

Thanks as always to the crew at Kensington; my editor, John Scognamiglio; and the teams in marketing and production. And to my agent, John Talbot.

Finally, thank you to my family. Bill Carito, the most patient man in the universe; Rob, Sunny, and Viola Carito; and Kate, Luke, and Etta Donius. You are the most important people in the world to me.